Subscription to Murder

A Meadowood Mystery

Nancy M. Wade

Published in the United States

GARNAN Enterprises, LLC of Ohio.

Copyright 2025 by Nancy M. Wade

All Rights Reserved.

ISBN: E979-89919301-61

ISBN: 979-89919301-78

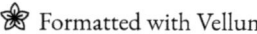 Formatted with Vellum

Cast of Characters

Meredith Gardner (Merry) – wife, mother of two boys, half-owner of A&M Tea Shop, and full-time amateur sleuth

Douglas Gardner - Merry's husband, sheriff of Meadowood, Army veteran, graduate of OSU, and former football player

Colleen Callahan Wythe - Elementary school principal, Merry's childhood friend and occasional sleuthing partner

Frances Andrews - Mayor of Meadowood, owner of Frannie's Frocks, and aunt to Merry

Anna Thompson – Merry's tea shop partner, good friend of both Merry & Fran, married to Chuck, hails from Texas

Trixie Jones – reporter & owner of Meadowood Flyer newspaper

Tony Dalton - deputy at sheriff's department

Carl Bradley, PhD – museum director hired by town council

Susan Moore – TN art museum director interviewed

Betty Jones – long-time sales girl at Frannie's Frocks, newly promoted to store manager

Cast of Characters

Georgia Simmons – wife of retired sheriff Edgar Simmons, city council secretary & hiring committee

Byron Adams – original museum director

Contents

Subscription to Murder

A Meadowood Mystery

Book 8

NANCY M. WADE

Chapter One

News

"Extra! Extra! Read all about it!" shouted the two boys as they ran down Meadowood's business district handing out papers to surprised citizens. Their voices rang out in the crisp autumn air.

I stepped out of the tea shop and watched the nostalgic newsies in their cute vintage 1940s clothing. Each boy worked a side of the street with a bundle of flyers tucked under his arm. The boys were dressed straight out of an old movie with their newsboy flat caps and flannel shirts tucked into tweed knickerbocker pants held up by a pair of wide suspenders. Knee socks and scuffed brown leather shoes completed the ensemble. If I didn't know better, I'd swear I was watching characters from a 1930s Thin Man movie.

Snapping pictures of both boys with my cell phone as they announced their news and made their way down the street, I eagerly awaited my copy to *read all about it*. Finally, one of the boys handed me the paper and tipped his hat to me as he hurried off.

I rubbed my arms to warm myself as I stepped back into our cozy tea shop with its chintz upholstered seats and floral wreaths decorating the walls. Sprigs of white mums in tiny vases decorated our tabletops. Lingering aromas of Earl Grey tea and warm spices filled the air. The atmosphere of our shop was quaint, feminine and inviting.

"What's all the commotion about?" Anna asked in her droll Texan twang.

Chuck and Anna Thompson had moved to Ohio from the panhandle of Texas about twelve years ago. Chuck's company had given him an ultimatum ... make the move or take an early retirement. Personally, I was extremely glad they had made the move. Anna was a true gem with her practical common sense and Western humor. She had become like a family member to me. Her son, Stevie, and my boys were inseparable friends.

Anna and I had bought the A&M Tea Shop over a year ago and had devoted all of our energy since then to growing our little enterprise into a popular tourist attraction within Meadowood. We served a variety of flavorful teas using delicate porcelain tea sets and miniature teapots. The local bakery, owned by our dear friend Martha Parker, provided delicious scones for our customers' delight. We supplemented our sweet offerings with muffins and cookies baked by Anna and me in the shop's kitchen plus a variety of tiny tea sandwiches. Display cases filled with knit tea cozies, delicate demitasse teacups, and a collection of sugar bowls and creamers tweaked our customer's interest and boosted our sales.

My eyes skimmed the brief article as a grin curled my lips. I handed my partner the printed broadsheet.

"What a clever idea. Looks like our friend Trixie Jones has opened her own newspaper. She couldn't have announced the event any better," I said.

Anna nodded and drawled, "Well! If that don't beat all! She never said a thing. We've got to go check this out."

"I agree. It's almost closing time. What do you say we close up shop early today and wander on down to the Meadowood Flyer's office?"

"Good idea. My curiosity is burning a hole in me," Anna drawled in that Texan accent of hers.

We quickly finished our closing procedures, slipped on warm jackets, then flipped the closed sign on the door and locked it behind us as we dashed out onto the street. The air had just an amount of bite to it to signal colder weather was on its way. Bronze and golden leaves swirled in the light breeze, falling from rows of maple and oak trees that lined the avenue. They scattered and crunched under our hurrying footsteps. We passed local businesses decorated for Halloween, all occupying Meadowood's brick and clapboard buildings, complete with dormers and gables on two-or three-story high roofs.

I glanced in store windows and waved to friendly faces as we made our way down the street. Meadowood is a picturesque town dating back two hundred years, with historic buildings that draw tourists to our rural community. It was the illusion of stepping back in time plus the friendliness of the townsfolk that people sought and which brought them back time after time. Meadowood evoked a sense of being at home, even if you were only a visitor.

Heading toward the location printed on the flyer, we passed my aunt's dress shop, Frannie's Frocks. Frances Andrews clutched a flyer in her gloved hand as she rushed outside to join us.

"Are you two headed where I think you are?" she asked as she fell into step with us.

"Madam Mayor, did you know about this new enterprise?" I asked. My aunt had been elected the town's mayor a year ago. As both a business owner and the mayor, she stayed a busy woman.

"I heard Trixie had come down to the city building to file for a permit and business license, but I didn't know it was for a newspaper. I'm intrigued, to say the least. Why would that gal give up her job at the Knox County Tribune?" Fran asked.

Traversing another block found us standing in front of a narrow brick three-story building with a wide plate-glass window that overlooked the street. The name *Meadowood Flyer* was stenciled onto the glass in gold letters. We entered the door; a schoolhouse bell jangled above the entrance, loudly announcing our arrival.

Trixie Jones stood behind a low counter that separated the painted buttercup yellow room into two spaces. She greeted us with a wide smile and a wave of her hand, inviting us inside. Two colonial spindle-backed wooden chairs sat along the front wall with a potted Ficus tree in the corner. Trixie's spacious desk occupied the area behind the counter with her computer and keyboard. It was littered with a pile of folders on one corner. Behind her, a wall of base cabinets supported printers, copiers, and stacked reams of paper. A brightly painted wooden sign proclaiming *Meadowood Flyer* in tall red letters hung on the wall, facing visitors as they entered.

"Ladies, welcome to the Flyer," Trixie said with a flourish.

We all started speaking at once. Above the volume of voices, Fran managed to be heard.

"Care to explain what this is all about?"

Trixie took a deep breath and faced the mayor and her friends. "I quit my job at the Tribune and now as you can see ... I'm reporter, editor, and publisher of Meadowood's own newspaper. It will be a weekly edition to start. I don't think I can manage a daily right now, but maybe in the future. Who knows?"

"Jeez Louise! I recall you told us you were buying the old podiatrist office, but I never expected this," I said as I glanced around. "Are you living here too?"

"Upstairs. I've got two floors above the shop that make a comfy living space. Full kitchen and good sized living room plus two bedrooms and a bath. Took some work to remodel the kitchen to my liking but the office space on the first floor was simple enough. All I had to do was rearrange the work area to give me shelving for storage. It's not like I have to fit in an industrial printer with lead typesetting. I'm not going full on vintage. I'll be creating the newspaper digitally on the computer and printing off copies."

"Can you make a living with this?" I asked.

"I think so. At least, I hope so. I'll sell advertising to local merchants, which I hope you'll support, and subscriptions to folks. I'm not a complete fool; I won't get rich doing this. But I've always wanted to run my own show. And now I get the chance. Meadowood is full of history and heaven knows it gets its share of excitement. From the short time I've been here, I've seen proof of that. There's plenty to write about," Trixie said.

"Well, I suppose congratulations are in order," Anna said.

"You're doing Meadowood a service. The town needs our own paper. I think folks will approve of your venture. That is ... as long as your idea isn't for a gossip sheet and scandalous lies," Fran warned.

"Absolutely not, Madam Mayor. Only truthful, accurate coverage of current events ... I promise. My first front page will show-case the new history museum." Trixie smiled at us, then invited us upstairs to see her home.

"Well, what do you think?" I asked my aunt as we sipped our coffee and enjoyed one of Martha Parker's delicious apple pies.

I had invited my aunt to share dinner with my family that night; a large beef pot roast I had slow-cooked in a crock pot during the day. Now we sat back with full tummies and relaxed over dessert. My sons, Billy and Johnny, had rushed upstairs to play video games before bedtime, leaving the adults to savor the peaceful evening.

"I hope she can make a go of it," Aunt Fran said. "Really, I meant it when I said the town could benefit from our own newspaper. Let folks post news about Meadowood events, kid's school achievements, upcoming holiday sales. Things like that. I'll certainly place an ad for the dress shop and I'm sure you'll want to advertise the tea shop. Won't you?"

"Definitely. Anna and I will support the paper. I just hope Trixie finds enough newsworthy topics to put in the paper."

Doug sat quietly listening to our discussion. I raised my eyebrow and shot him a look, asking for his input. My husband knew me so well. He leaned back in his chair and took a sip of his coffee.

"Miss Jones has already approached my office and asked if the sheriff's department would like to do a weekly column. Like some kind of police beat. I told her I'd think about it."

"Really? I think that could be a good thing. Don't you? Would you write it or delegate the task to someone in the office?" I asked Doug.

"I dunno. Guess I could jot down some notes. Depends on how busy we get. As sheriff, I have more pressing duties than just posting bulletins about some cat up a tree," Doug said with a snort of laughter.

"Of course, dear. I know you do."

With a final grunt, Doug got up and carried his dessert plate and mug into the kitchen. I heard him turn on the TV in the living room before settling down in his recliner as a fire crackled in the hearth.

I turned my attention back to my aunt. She smiled, and we both held in our laughter as silent communication passed between us. It wasn't the first time we'd read each other's minds, with no words needed. Our relationship of aunt and niece was uniquely close. Sometimes I think I'm closer to my aunt than my mother. We even looked like each other with our blue-gray eyes and blond hair. Of course, Fran's hair is longer with strands of gray in it while mine is short and curly, but that's the only difference.

"Have you heard from your mother? I bet she and William are relishing their cruise," Aunt Fran said as she cleared her dishes.

I followed her into the kitchen with the last of the pie. After stacking the dishwasher with the soiled plates and cups, I finished the cleanup by wiping down the granite countertop.

Grabbing a plastic container from the cabinet, I ladled the remaining beef and gravy into the container, added a heaping spoonful of sliced carrots, onions, and potatoes then snapped the lid shut. The empty pot went into the sink to soak in hot soapy water.

"Here's supper for tomorrow ... or lunch. Only enough left over for one serving. You enjoy it."

I slid the food container toward her. Reaching for my cell phone, I scrolled through my text messages until I found the one from my mother.

"Mom sent this pic of her and Dad. Get a load of the outfits. She says it was doo wop night and everyone had to dress like the 1950s. I have no idea where she found that poodle skirt but they seem to be having a blast."

Fran studied the photo on my phone and smiled. "I'm glad. Appears the two of them are behaving like newlyweds again. Nice to see after that fiasco with that creepy dinosaur professor two years ago. My sister is lucky her husband is so forgiving."

I nodded as I looked at the picture again. My parents were smiling lovingly at each other as the camera captured the moment.

"How's Betty managing at the store?" I asked.

"I couldn't be more pleased. She's really stepped up with the promotion to store manager and since I'm more involved with mayoral duties these days, it's been a blessing. Betty wants to hire a high school gal part time to help with the stocking and duties Betty used to do. I told her to go ahead; I trust her judgement."

"That's great. With the holiday season approaching, you'll be getting even busier at the store and can use the help."

"We've already seen an increase in business. I'm certainly not complaining but it puts a strain on staffing. I've got to try to be in the shop more but until I get this museum opened up and running, it's been consuming all my time. You know how much this project means to me. It was one of my campaign promises and I just have to make good on it," Fran said. She stared out the kitchen window as if willing herself to see the future.

"Don't worry. The museum will open and it will be fantastic."

"I hope you're right. Well kiddo, thanks for the delicious meal and the leftovers. I've got to get a move on. There's a town council meeting early in the morning and I'm interviewing potential directors for the museum."

"Let me know if I can do anything to help with the grand opening of the Meadowood history museum," I said as I walked her to the door.

I stood watching the full moon slide in and out of gray clouds, casting its meager light. Leaves floated on a light wind, covering the ground in russet colors. Soon it would be snow blanketing the earth; winter weather was knocking on our door. Change was in the air. I could feel it.

Chapter Two

Council Plans

Mayor Frances Andrews tapped the gavel on a wooden block to bring the meeting to order. She glanced around the cavernous room with its rich walnut paneling and made a note of who sat in attendance.

"All right everyone. Settle down. Let's begin by hearing the minutes from our board secretary. Mrs. Simmons, if you would be so kind," Fran said with a nod to the robust woman.

Georgia Simmons, silver-haired, sharp-tongued, and a stalwart pillar of the community, stood up and read from her carefully typed notes. The wife of retired Sheriff Edgar Simmons as well as the past president of the PTA, Georgia was accustomed to public speaking. With her voice commanding attention, she made eye contact with the members seated around the board room.

"... the council voted in a seven to two majority to schedule the museum opening for the week of October twentieth," she finished.

"Thank you, Georgia. As you know, the town's historical museum is a pet project of mine and I'm thrilled to see it finally come to fruition. We delayed the opening due to the sudden resignation of our director, Byron Adams. However, I am interviewing three candidates today that the board selected from the list of applicants. I'm hopeful we can immediately hire a new director to replace Adams and oversee the final touches to the museum in time for its grand opening. This museum represents the story of Meadowood and its people, dating back to colonial times when this land was only a territory. I'm proud to honor my campaign promise to promote tourism and build revenue for our citizen businesses with the opening of this museum."

A round of applause erupted at the end of the mayor's speech. Colleen raised her hand and waited to be acknowledged.

"Thank you. The chair recognizes our school principal, Colleen Wythe," Fran stated, then pointed to Colleen to rise.

Colleen faced the council members. "I'm chairman of our annual food drive for the homeless. Chief Lawson has offered the fire station again as a collection point for the food drive. This year, I'd like to suggest that we also hold a fund raising event to coincide with the new museum's grand opening."

"What did you have in mind?" asked Patsy Malone of Stems and Petals Florist.

Colleen glanced toward Fran. She nodded for her to continue. Taking a breath, Colleen slowly exhaled and then faced the room, hoping her idea would be met with enthusiasm.

"In keeping with the season, since Halloween will come up soon, I, um, thought a masquerade party would be fun. An adults only affair with ticket prices going toward money for the food bank. The renovations are completed on the adjacent Methodist church next to the museum. It's ready for use as the city's event venue or conference center. I think this fund raising party would be the perfect occasion to kick off the new venue. With minimal decorations, it would be ready in no time. We could ask everyone to come as a favorite historic figure or maybe a character from a movie or book. You know, historic characters to commemorate a historic museum." Colleen studied the faces before her, trying to judge their reaction.

A few people smiled and nodded; others looked confused.

Michael Sullivan, owner of the Gas and Go station and convenience store, tentatively raised his hand with a question.

"Let me get this straight. You want us to dress up like somebody from the movies?" Sullivan asked as he scratched his head.

Colleen turned to him and tried to explain. "Meadowood is a historic town. We all agree on that, right? So let's celebrate the history of our town by dressing as people who lived when Meadowood was founded or maybe from other periods of time. For instance, someone could dress as pioneers who settled the Ohio territory; wear clothes like in Laura Ingalls "Little House on the Prairie". Maybe come as your favorite movie character from the 1930s when Meadowood was involved in prohibition like the rest of the country. Think Bonnie and Clyde or Al Capone. It's easy to get ideas if you think of your favorite movie or literary character and how they dressed."

"Oh, I get it. Sounds like fun. Can we have a speakeasy inside the new banquet hall?" asked Patsy.

"That would be a clever idea instead of the usual buffet and refreshments," Fran said.

"We'd want this event to be restricted to adults only because of the alcoholic drinks that will be served. Children can trick or treat for Halloween two days after the museum party and have their fun. This night will give the grownups a chance to howl," Colleen said with a wide grin, and everyone on the council laughed.

Fran tapped the gavel again to silence the room and conclude the meeting.

"Ladies and gentlemen, Colleen will coordinate with those of you volunteering to work on her party committee. We'll need help selling the tickets. I'm posting a sign-up sheet for anyone who can help with the museum open house too as guides or greeters at the door. You can find that at the city building's front reception desk. If there is no other business, may I have a motion to adjourn the meeting?"

Colleen stood and stated, "I move we adjourn the meeting."

Bill Carr, from Carr's Hardware Store, spoke up and said, "I second that motion."

"All right. Thank you, everyone, for attending today and for your excellent suggestions. This town council meeting is officially adjourned. I have candidate interviews this afternoon then will convene with the hiring committee afterwards to discuss a selection," Fran said.

Everyone stood and filed out of the room. Fran glanced at her watch and checked her typed agenda.

"I've got time for a quick lunch before my first interview if I hurry."

Colleen, who had stayed behind, walked out of the conference room with the mayor.

"How about we pop into the tea shop for a quick sandwich? You know Merry will be dying to find out about the masquerade party," Colleen said.

"Call her and tell her we're on our way so she can have something plated. I've got to eat and run."

"All set," Colleen said as she clicked off her cell phone and they walked the short distance to the A&M Tea Shop.

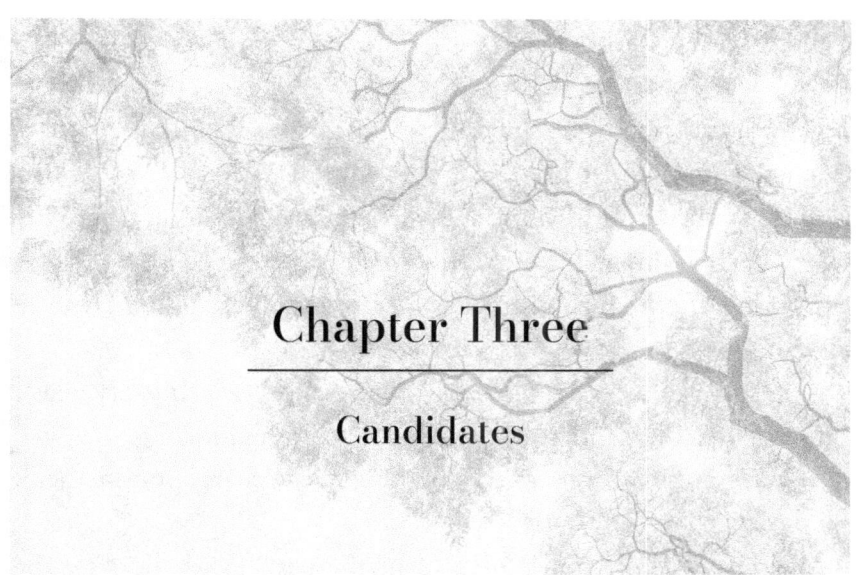

Chapter Three

Candidates

F ran adjusted the brooch on her lapel, a delicate magnolia blossom carved from ivory, a gift from her late husband. She leaned back in her chair; seated behind the carved mahogany desk in the mayor's office within Meadowood's town hall. A tidy stack of résumés sat before her with a steaming hot cup of coffee beside it.

"Remind me again, Georgia," Fran murmured to her companion as she flipped through the stack of résumés, "why we need a marketing degree to run a history museum?"

Georgia Simmons squeezed her girth into a comfortable armchair to the side of the desk. She snorted. "I'm still trying to figure out why he listed *TikTok strategist* under special skills, but the committee selected him as a finalist."

Fran arched a brow. "Lord help us."

Just then, the door creaked open. Dottie, the receptionist and mayor's secretary, poked her head in. "First candidate's here. Sending him in."

. . .

Candidate #1 – Carl Bradley

He was a studious-looking man in his late forties, thin and pale. Tall, slightly stooped shoulders, he wore a blazer with leather elbow patches, wire-rimmed glasses, and the unmistakable air of a man who'd spent most of his adult life in an archive. He stood before the two women, waiting for an invitation to be seated.

"Good afternoon, Dr. Bradley," Fran greeted, standing to shake his hand.

"Please, call me Carl," he replied, his voice warm but dry, like a classroom lecture that had gone just a few minutes too long.

"Have a seat," Georgia said, gesturing to the chair opposite them. "Tell us, why Meadowood?"

Carl folded his hands. "I've spent the past decade heading the history department at Fairview College. But academic life can grow ... stale. I've always admired smaller communities that take pride in their roots. When I read about the Society of Free Men artifacts being moved to the new museum, I thought ... this is a rare chance to shape history for a living audience."

Fran exchanged a quick glance with Georgia, intrigued.

"The Society of Free Men? I'm surprised you know of that secret organization," Fran shot the candidate a pointed look.

"Of course I do. Why wouldn't I?" Bradley responded.

"Well, because it was secret. I didn't learn of it until last year and I live here. I find it puzzling that you were aware of its existence."

"I, uh, must have read about it in the newspaper last year."

"Uh-huh, and your vision for the museum?" Fran asked.

Carl cleared his throat. He recited as if by memory, a historical shopping list. "Chronological exhibitions highlighting Meadowood's role in Ohio's settlement, early industry, and the Civil War. Interactive timelines. Showcase the artifacts from the Society of Free Men. And possibly a lecture series—monthly talks on local history, primary sources, perhaps create a historical fiction book club to engage younger folks."

"Book club?" Georgia brightened. "Now you're speaking my language."

Carl smiled faintly. He recognized the woman's soft spot and sought to take advantage. "Historical accuracy is important—but so is keeping the public engaged. I imagine you, dear lady, are no stranger to that concept."

Georgia giggled and preened under his glowing comment. "What about your availability? We want someone who can oversee the opening of the museum and be ready to take charge by next week. Will that be a problem for you?"

He raised an eyebrow, swallowed audibly ... his Adam's apple bobbing up and down. "Um, yes, I suppose I could do that. It isn't much notice."

Fran nodded. "We understand. Unfortunately circumstances have necessitated the short time frame. Thank you, Dr. Bradley. We'll be in touch."

As he exited, Georgia leaned toward Fran. "Solid credentials. He reminds me of my dear nephew, Jacob. He'd bring prestige."

Fran scribbled: *Knows his stuff. Needs sparkle? Weird reaction to the S.O.F.M. Gives me an uneasy feeling.*

Fran sipped her coffee and glanced at the clock. These interviews made her think of the speed dating young people engaged in these days. She sighed. This certainly wasn't the best way to hire someone for a prestigious position ... hardly enough time to thoroughly vet an individual. Dottie rapped on the door, then ushered in the next person.

Candidate #2 – Susan Moore

The next candidate entered with a polished air, manicured nails, and a portfolio under one arm. A tortoise-shell clip held her sable brown hair twisted into a smooth chignon. Light makeup and a subdued lip gloss provided a soft classical appearance. Susan Moore, 40, a former art museum director, wore a fitted navy wool dress and spectator pumps. She carried herself like someone used to fundraising galas and boardroom battles.

"Mayor Andrews, Mrs. Simmons, thank you for this opportunity."

"Please, sit down," Fran said. "You've run a museum before?"

"Yes, the Sevier Museum of Art in Tennessee for twelve years. But my first love has always been American history. I went back for a second master's in history while working at Sevier. What appeals to me about Meadowood is its rich pioneer legacy — and the fact that the community is ready to curate and preserve its own story."

Georgia raised a skeptical brow, studying the composed and attractive woman in front of her. She squirmed in her seat, suddenly feeling awkward and frumpy. "Wouldn't you miss the art world?"

Susan gave a charming laugh. "History is art, Mrs. Simmons. Every artifact tells a story. Every archive is a canvas. Besides, I've spent enough time chasing down eccentric collectors and wrangling grant committees to last a lifetime. I'd love the challenge of displaying Meadowood's rich history while creating a destination for both tourists and locals alike to visit and explore."

Fran liked her poise. And her sass. "You'd be dealing with a small-town board of volunteers. Bake sale fundraisers instead of wine tastings."

Susan grinned. "Honey, I can raise money with a raffle, a goat, and a crockpot of chili. Just point me to the church basement."

Georgia chuckled. "Those talents might be needed."

"What about our timeline? Would you be able to step in with only a week's notice? Events have dictated the need for our new museum director to hit the floor running, so to speak," the mayor stated.

"Yes. Absolutely. I've left my post in Tennessee and I am more than able to relocate to Meadowood immediately," Moore said.

"Thank you Miss Moore. We'll be notifying applicants by tomorrow evening," Fran said.

Susan Moore stood, smiled at each of the women as she shook their hands then left.

Fran underlined her notes twice: *Sharp. Capable. Could out-talk me on a good day. I like her.*

Candidate #3 – Gilbert Farrow

Their final candidate bounded into the office like a golden retriever let off its leash. Stocky in build, with tousled sandy brown hair, he wore a wrinkled shirt and corduroy pants. Farrow looked like an athlete straight off a football field or a boy about to meet his date's parents for the first time.

"Hi! I'm Gilbert Farrow. Call me Gil." He thrust out his hand enthusiastically, nearly toppling Georgia's glass of water.

"Careful, son," Fran said, recovering the glass. "No need to hydrate the interview panel."

Gil laughed. "Sorry! Nervous energy. I just graduated from Kenyon College with my master's in marketing. This would be my first real job, and I'm *so* excited to bring fresh ideas to Meadowood!"

Georgia blinked. "You ... don't have a background in history?"

"Well, not officially. But I created an entire project on branding historic towns for my thesis. I created a mock social media campaign for a fictional village in colonial Virginia—'History You Can Hashtag.'"

Fran sighed.

"Imagine this," Gil continued. "QR codes on exhibits. An escape room in the basement based on a Civil War gold conspiracy. A 'Museum After Dark' series with themed wine nights ... Scandals & History. I can make Meadowood trend on Instagram."

"I'm not even sure what half those words mean," Georgia muttered.

Fran was trying hard not to laugh. "Gil ... this is a town where people still call the grocery store 'the A&P' even though it closed in '97."

"Exactly," Gil said brightly. "Untapped charm. Total brand goldmine."

As he left the room, Georgia turned to Fran. "If he ends up running the place, I want you to know I'll be faking an allergy to hashtags."

Fran smiled. "But admit it, he'd have that museum packed with tourists under thirty."

"I'll give him points for youthful enthusiasm. And maybe breathlessness; heaven help us!"

Fran tapped her pencil against her notes. Three candidates, three wildly different visions.

"Well," she said, stacking the résumés, "do we want a scholar, an art visionary, or a social media whirlwind?"

Georgia leaned back in her chair. "I think we want a director who can honor the past and bring us into the future without scaring off the ladies' quilting guild."

Fran sighed. "Lord help us. Maybe we need all three."

Later in the council chambers ...

The setting sun colored the high windows of the Meadowood Town Hall, casting long amber streaks across the oak-paneled walls of the council chamber. Radiators rattled as warm steam heat filled the room and warded off the October chill. Outside, the wind blew and bare tree branches scratched the window panes.

The mayor, seated at the center of the long dais, adjusted her reading glasses and tapped the gavel once to call the meeting to order. Around her, the council hiring committee gathered—five members seated in faux-leather rolling chairs around the conference table.

The agenda was short. One item: the final vote to appoint the director of the new Meadowood History Museum.

Georgia and Fran each shared their notes and impressions from the interviews of the candidates in question. The council members reviewed all the résumé copies. Members put their heads together and discussed the qualifications they had read. Fingers pointed to key references, and heads nodded. The clock on the wall ticked away the hours.

Councilwoman Georgia Simmons leaned toward the microphone. She directed her comments to those members more malleable. "Before we vote, I'd just like to say ... I think any of our three candidates could do a fine job. But only one of them truly understands the *history* part of the history museum." Sitting back, she shot Bill a pointed look.

Councilman Bill Carr, a proud alumni of Meadowood High class of '72, nodded. "Carl Bradley's got the book learnin'. A Ph.D. doesn't grow on trees, ya know."

Councilwoman Tonya Perez, the youngest on the panel and a local elementary school teacher, gave a measured shrug. "I liked Susan Moore. She has spark and appreciates the artistic value of our artifacts. Her experience running an art museum would be beneficial. Plus she seemed like she could organize things, showcase our town's history while fundraising too."

Fran held her expression neutral as she recorded notes while agreeing with Tonya one-hundred percent. But she'd been mayor long enough to know when a decision had already taken shape ... and she felt this one had.

Finally, after a brief procedural review, the votes were cast by show of hands. Carl Bradley received the majority, totaling three of the five votes. Only Tonya and Fran had voted for Susan Moore. Gilbert Farrow, to no one's surprise, received none, although Fran suspected Georgia had flirted with the idea just to add chaos.

The motion passed. Carl Bradley would be the new museum director. Fran would make a phone call in the morning offering him the position.

Fran tapped the gavel again and gave the official announcement. A polite round of applause followed. The session ended without fanfare, and the council members, yawning, trickled out with murmurs of "well, that's that" and "we'll see how he does."

The clock chimed ten o'clock; Fran Andrews curled up on one end of her teal patterned sofa that faced a pair of comfortable chocolate-brown suede club chairs. She closed her eyes and sighed, needing the peace and quiet after the hectic day she'd had. Fran's living room had an almost Zen mystique about it, focusing on the tranquil ocean scene hanging above her fireplace. The painting was one of the few possessions she had brought back from California after her husband had died years earlier. Studying the artwork with its turquoise and aqua colors — visions of silky sand, the taste of salt air, the feel of the ebb tide, and the sounds of hypnotic waves rushing toward the lonely beach permeated your senses.

I sat across from her, my legs tucked under me in the comfy club chair, waiting to hear her news.

"So, Carl Bradley got the job?" I asked, tucking a strand of hair behind my ear. After finishing dinner and saying goodnight to my boys, I had rushed over to my aunt's home, curious about how the vote had gone.

Fran exhaled slowly. "Yes, he did. Georgia led the charge. She had made up her mind before we ever met with the board. You know how she can get; obstinate and used to getting her own way."

"Oh, I know. She can be a real pain. When she was president of the parent teachers' association, I wanted to kill her on more than one occasion. That is one bossy woman. Did the men cower?"

"Oh yes. Bill Carr followed like he always does. And Michael Sullivan sided with Bill, keeping the male vote united."

I smiled. "Ah. Nothing like united testosterone."

Fran chuckled but then sobered. She swirled the wine in her glass. "Thing is ... Merry... I wanted Susan Moore. I know she's from out of state and majored in art, but she had the right mix of experience and energy. That woman could've turned the museum into something special."

Tilting my head, I studied my aunt. "Then why didn't you push harder for her?"

"I tried. But a mayor only nudges. If I push too hard, they dig in their heels. Besides..." She sighed and leaned back. "It wouldn't have mattered. Georgia had already labeled Carl *director* three times before the vote."

I frowned. "So what's bothering you?"

Fran hesitated, her brow furrowing. "Something about him doesn't sit right. He answered everything correctly. Too correctly. Like he rehearsed the town's entire history from a brochure."

"That's what good candidates do," I offered gently.

"Sure. But he had this ... detachment. Like he wasn't *invested*. His smile didn't reach his eyes, and when I asked him about the Society of Free Men artifacts, he got cagey. Dodged the specifics. Made me wonder about his interest in the S.O.F.M.

"That could be nerves. The society is disbanded; there shouldn't be any danger from them now."

Fran nodded, but slowly. "Maybe. But when I shook his hand, Merry, I felt it in my bones. He's hiding something. I just can't put my finger on what."

I leaned forward, setting my wine glass aside. "Do you want me to do a little digging? Quietly? You said these candidates weren't really fully vetted. What's this guy's background? I can check him out."

Fran studied me. A soft smile touched her lips. Our eyes met, reading each other's minds in silent communication.

"No, not yet. Let's give him a chance. Maybe I'm being overly cautious. The committee saw something in him they liked. Perhaps I'm just being biased and wanted a woman in the job."

I didn't push. My aunt knew I would do whatever she needed. I had a knack for stumbling into trouble and solving it.

Outside, a breeze stirred the porch swing, and somewhere down the block, a dog barked into the chilly night. I pulled my coat tighter around me as I made my way back home.

Fran watched the moon rise over the rooftops of Meadowood. She couldn't shake the feeling that they had just handed the keys to the museum ... and maybe more, to someone who wasn't quite who he claimed to be.

And if Meadowood had taught her anything, it was that secrets never stayed buried for long.

Chapter Four

Fall Buzz

Days flew by like autumn leaves in a whirlwind. All around town, Meadowood reflected the fall season with artful arrangements of corn stalks and pumpkins atop bales of straw in front of town hall or shops displaying decorative bunches of fall leaves and gourds in front windows. Tourists strolled downtown, bought delicious spicy carrot cakes and pumpkin breads from Martha's bakery, browsed the latest fall clothing in Frannie's Frocks, or explored the unique pottery made in kilns at the edge of town. Our tea shop stayed busy as folks found their way to our little cottage to quench their thirsts and soak in the cozy peacefulness.

Anna and I bustled back and forth between the dining area and our kitchen. Trying a new recipe, Anna had baked mozzarella cheese cubes, rolled in an Italian seasoned coating of breadcrumbs and baked just until the creamy cheese melted. She served the cheesy bites along with tea sandwiches spread with a mixture of sun-dried tomatoes and cream cheese on toasted Italian bread. It soon became a popular luncheon selection along with our traditional shredded chicken salad or tuna salad sandwiches. The sandwiches, along with a sweet treat, hit the spot after a morning spent shopping.

I plated raisin bran muffins, sweet cinnamon scones, and ginger spice cupcakes on a tiered stand. Anna added a delicate porcelain teapot filled with steeping chai tea flavored with hints of orange. Balancing the tray of tea and baked goods, I served a table of four older women. They had arrived with a church tour group on a day trip from Mt. Vernon. Several shopping bags lay at their feet.

"Are you ladies enjoying your day?" I asked as I poured them each a cup of tea. Placing ramekins of butter, jam, and sweet whipped cream on the table, I set the tiered selection of baked goods in the center.

"We've had a delightful day. I never knew Meadowood had so many darling shops," one lady commented.

Her companion, a silver-haired woman wearing a pale blue wool coat with a fox collar, nodded in agreement. "I understand a new museum is opening soon. Do you know anything about that?"

"Yes. Meadowood has created a history museum to celebrate the Ohio territory, the early settlers who founded our town, and to honor the history of Meadowood through the generations. The director, Doctor Carl Bradley, has been working with local volunteers to ready the exhibits for a grand opening in two days."

"Oh my, that sounds interesting. We'll have to come back."

"Please do. There'll be a celebration and open house at the museum on Friday, and later that night, a masquerade ball is planned. Everyone in town is looking forward to it," I said.

"My goodness! How exciting," the women chimed in.

Around town, ticket sales for the party were selling like hot cakes. We had sold all our ticket coupons in the shop. I couldn't help but wonder if everyone would actually fit inside the old Methodist church that was being used as the party venue. A huge turnout was expected.

The bell above our door jingled as Barb Williams and Carol Goodwin came into the shop. I waved a hello and pointed to a small table by the window for them to be seated.

"Hey gals, what's up?" I asked.

"Just thought I'd pop in for a quick snack plus I wanted to ask what you're wearing to the party Friday night?" asked Barbara.

"Give me a minute and I'll be back with some tea and muffins for you gals," I said as I hurried back into the kitchen.

"Barb and Carol just popped in. They want to know what we're wearing to the party?" I told Anna as I prepared a pot of Earl Grey tea and plates of raisin bran muffins for them.

"Good question. I'm not sure Chuck and I have decided either," Anna said. She wiped her hands on a towel and joined me as we served our friends. One glance around the shop assured me we had only the last table of tourists present. When they finished, I cashed out the ladies, then took a seat at Barb's table.

"Doug wants to dress as Dick Tracy so I guess I'll come up with some kind of outfit to play his girlfriend Tess Trueheart. You know Doug, he's got to be some type of lawman," I laughed.

"Well, if Colleen wants us to be a historic or movie figure, I reckon Chuck and I could be Roy Rodgers and Dale Evans. Won't have any problems rounding up some western gear to wear," Anna said with a chuckle and her best Texan drawl.

"Oh, those are fun costumes," Carol said, reaching for a bran muffin. "I was thinking of Pete dressing as Dudley Do-Right and I could be his Nell Fenwick. Does that sound too corny?"

"I can just picture fireman Pete in a Mountie's uniform. He'd be perfect. But where are you going to find the red uniform?" I asked.

"Oh that won't be a problem. He's got a cousin that lives in Zanesville who used to be a Canadian Mountie. Harry told Pete he'd loan him the jacket and hat; they're about the same size."

"Wow! That's fantastic," Barb commented. "Now I'm really stumped for a theme for Ted and me. You've all got great ideas."

"Why not come as private eye Mike Hammer and his girl Friday? You can wear anything slinky and Ted just needs a wide tie and a fedora hat to complete the image," I suggested.

"Oh, I like that idea. Thanks, Merry. Are you all planning on wearing a mask?" Barb asked.

"Probably. Maybe one of those Mardi Gras half things that just covers your eyes and nose. I'm not sure I'll keep it on for the entire night," I said.

"Super! Guess we better finish up so you gals can close for the day. Are you attending the open house for the museum too?" Carol asked as she finished her tea and wiped her mouth with a napkin.

"Anna and I plan to close the tea shop for the entire day so we can attend the museum open house then get ready for the party later. I don't imagine we'd have much business anyway with all the hub-bub going on at the other end of town."

"Well, see you there," Barb said as she and Carol left, and I locked the door behind them.

Anna and I cleared tables, whipped up salads for the next day's menu, then placed them in the refrigerator and tallied the sales for the day.

"I'll drop off our receipts at the bank. I want to pop into the Flyer's office and give Trixie our advertising copy," I told Anna as I wiped down our preparation counter. I gathered up linen napkins and tea towels into a bundle to launder at home later tonight.

"Okay. See you tomorrow," Anna said as we both left by the back door and locked up our tea shop.

I drove the four blocks down to the newspaper office. Parking on the street, I dashed into the bank next door to make our deposit first. The bank tellers waited to assist customers; it was still the lull before the hectic late afternoon banking business when swarms of employees cashed paychecks and shop owners along Park Drive deposited their day's sales. We'd had a string of store break-ins last year, and now most businesses continued the cautious habit of depositing their cash before closing and avoiding any large amount of money kept in their registers overnight.

Finished with my banking, I entered the newspaper office. Trixie had her head down, concentrating on a layout of advertising copy and columns of text, juggling the pieces like a large jig-saw puzzle.

"Be right with you," she said without looking up.

I waited, fascinated with her editing galley proofs. "No problem. I'll wait," I said.

Trixie's head snapped up, recognizing my voice. "Oh, hey. I'll just be a second."

Trixie moved over to the counter where I waited. Her clothes were messy, and she had a streak of black toner along her cheek, but the grin she wore proclaimed her happiness. I couldn't help but return her smile, knowing my new friend had found her calling.

"I want to place an ad for the tea shop," I told her. "Here's what Anna and I want in the ad. You can arrange it as you like, as long as you include these details." I slid a typed note to her.

Trixie read the information and nodded. "Okay, I think a two by three ad size will work best. That's two columns wide and three inches long. Like this," she said and grabbed the galley proof she had been working with to point to a rectangular box.

"What's the cost for an ad that size?"

"Do you plan on keeping the ad in the paper each week or just run it once?" asked Trixie.

"Well since the Flyer is only a weekly, I'd like the ad run in each edition. Make it a permanent ad; we can update details as needed for the holidays and stuff."

"Okay, I'll give you an annual subscription to the paper which includes the weekly ad. How about this? Sound affordable?" Trixie asked as she scribbled a figure onto my note.

I raised my eyebrow at the number. "Wow, I didn't realize advertising was so expensive."

"Remember, you're getting fifty-two ads. That's a full year. I normally charge a hundred dollars a column inch but since the paper is new plus you and Anna are friends, I'm giving you a fifty percent discount," Trixie said.

"Can I give Anna a call and get back to you on that price. Maybe we can pay half now and the other half in six months? Twenty-six hundred dollars for advertising is a major expense for us. I know that's the going rate and you're being fair, it's just that we have to look at our budget too. Can I run this ad in the next issue and then do a contract with you? See what kind of response we get from the ad? I think I'd be more comfortable with that idea," I said.

"Sure. That would work."

I breathed a sigh of relief. I didn't want to insult Trixie, but I couldn't agree to that kind of expense without checking with my partner.

"Hey, are you writing an article about the museum opening and the new director, by any chance?" I asked, changing the subject from advertising business.

"Yeah, front page news. Why?"

"Just wondering if you did any research on Carl Bradley ... his background and stuff," I said.

"Preliminary info, not a deep dive. Why? Do you think I might find something if I do? My reporter nose is starting to twitch. What do you know?"

"Nothing, really. Just a feeling. This is off the record, but my Aunt Fran said he acted odd when discussing the museum content and the S.O.F.M. He appeared to be particularly interested in that society. Maybe you can investigate him with some of your sources."

"What about you? You normally do a pretty complete job of researching individuals. Have you learned anything?"

"I've only looked at some basic information on him; nothing you couldn't find on Google. Maybe we can put our heads together on this project. He just doesn't feel right and I trust my instincts." I said.

"Okay. You got it. You are going to the open house on Friday and the party later, right?" Trixie asked.

"Of course. Doug and I will see you there."

I went home and threw on a load of laundry for the tea shop, then pulled out my laptop. Entering Carl Bradley's name into several search engines, it became apparent that the doctor didn't seem to exist before his tenure at Fairview College. How odd. I tried variations of his name, but no hits. His biography at Fairview listed academic certifications with the University of Pennsylvania, but when I searched the alumni records of that university, Bradley's name was not among them. Who was this guy?

Chapter Five

Open House

The Grand Opening of Meadowood's new history museum was the type of event that made the whole town buzz with excitement. Volunteers had worked tirelessly setting up exhibits. For weeks, the town had prepared for the event with flyers posted in every storefront: the bakery, hardware store, and especially the window of Frannie's Frocks. But seeing the building in person that morning – a stunning teal blue clapboard structure with wide brick steps and tall glass doors framed by black iron lanterns—was something else entirely. The committee had magically transformed the old parsonage of the abandoned Methodist church into a vessel to showcase our town's chronicles.

"Smells like fresh paint, antiques, and old books," I said to Doug as we stepped inside the double doors Friday morning. The Sheriff raised an eyebrow and smirked.

"You would know, Merry," he said, patting my shoulder. "You spend half your life sniffing around old attics and flea markets."

He wasn't wrong. My nose was as trained to spot precious antique teapots as his was to detect crime.

It seemed appropriate that the vacant parsonage had been converted into the museum, especially since a minister was one of the original settlers of Meadowood. Traveling preachers rode the rural paths of the Northwest Territory in the early 1800s, bringing both the word of God and civilization. One of those ministers chose to stay and founded the settlement that later became known as Meadowood.

The interior of the museum was bright and elegant, lit by hanging Edison bulbs and sunlight streaming through high windows. Glass display cases lined the walls, filled with artifacts dating back to the 1800s: dusty ledgers, bone-handled knives, hand-stitched quilts, even a pair of worn leather boots said to have belonged to Reverend Amos Kirkland, one of the original settlers of Meadowood. I couldn't help but feel a sense of pride as I inspected the exhibits showcasing my town. Meadowood. My home.

I stepped away from Doug to peer into another glass case. Faint lemon-scented furniture polish and aged paper floated on the air. A more enticing aroma of fresh hot cinnamon rolls brought me back.

"Is that Martha's work I smell?" asked Anna Thompson as she and her husband Chuck joined us near the refreshment table.

"Of course," I said. "No one bakes cinnamon twists like she does."

Martha Parker had outdone herself, laying out a spread of pastries, bite-sized quiches, and delicious cookies. Guests in suits and dresses mingled with locals in jeans and flannel, everyone sipping glasses of chilled apple cider.

I squeezed past a group of people, moving closer to my aunt's podium. Townsfolk crowded the museum; eager to get a look at all the fuss. I noticed several out of towners attending the open house too. My aunt would be pleased to learn the museum was already attracting tourists like she had hoped.

Aunt Fran, as mayor, stood on a small platform near the entrance, dressed in a burgundy-colored pantsuit with her signature string of pearls. Beside her stood the newly hired museum director, Dr. Carl Bradley.

The conservative director wore a navy blazer, khakis, and shiny brown loafers that looked brand new. He appeared ill at ease in the spotlight, making me wonder even more about his mysterious identity.

"Welcome citizens of Meadowood!" Fran called, tapping the mic. "Explore our town's glorious history. And be sure to return later tonight for the marvelous masquerade ball that kicks off our holiday season and supports the shelter's annual food drive."

Applause filled the air, and a few people whooped.

Carl stepped forward with a shy smile. "Thank you, Mayor Andrews. And thank you to the Historical Society for trusting me with this incredible collection. It's an honor to help preserve the legacy of Meadowood and our surrounding region, from Ohio's days as a wild territory to the bustling, proud community we are today."

He gestured toward a display with a dramatic flair I didn't expect. "You'll find personal items from Meadowood's founding families: the Kirkland, Johnson, and Maxwell families, as well as several newly acquired pieces from estate donations and historical archives." Bradley paused to take a breath; he stuttered slightly as he addressed the ensemble again. "Don't be shy. Explore, question, and most importantly ... take pride in your community."

Doug leaned close. "I hope this guy's better with old stuff than public speaking."

I grinned and took a sip of cider. "Maybe he's just nervous."

Georgia Simmons chatted with a group of women from her bridge club. I watched her preening and gesturing toward the new director, taking credit for his hiring.

"And I personally chose the man for the position. He has a doctorate in history, you know. We're so fortunate to have him," Georgia's voice carried throughout the front room.

Crowds of people strolled through the various rooms of the museum. I was glad to see an equal number of children interested in the relics on display as well as adults. It would make an excellent school field trip in the future.

Teresa Maxwell, sporting flaming orange hair, hung on the arm of her brother Alvin. Teresa owned the Cut & Curl salon and was famous for her changing flamboyant hair color plus her dedicated gossip communication network that rivaled any phone company. She had divorced her husband about seven years ago and resumed her maiden name of Maxwell. Looking at the display of founding fathers, I realized that Teresa's family must be related to those original Maxwells. I don't know why I never considered it before.

Wanting to greet the hairstylist, I stepped closer to her and Alvin. "Hey, Teresa! Were you looking for your family artifacts and history? You must be very proud," I said.

"Hmm, yes, well, Alvin told me he saw Maxwell memorabilia. Of course it's nice to know the family is represented as one of the founders," Teresa said, then moved on.

Trixie Jones stood off to the side with her reporter's notebook in hand, her dark brunette curls bouncing as she jotted things down. She caught my eye and winked. I waved back, knowing she'd already planned her headline: *Mystery and Memory Unveiled at Meadowood Museum.*

"I'm going to double-check security. I want to have a look at those window locks," Doug whispered in my ear. "I'll catch up with you later."

"Okay," I said as he moved through the crowd toward the rear of the building.

Wandering through the exhibits, I passed a glass case filled with hand-drawn maps, brittle pages showing the winding Ohio River, early boundary lines, and faded ink notations. I paused at a wooden writing desk tucked into the corner of the Pioneer Room. It was made of dark cherry, intricately carved, with brass pulls shaped like acorns. The rich wood patina gleamed.

A small placard read: Antique Writing Desk, ca. 1815.

Donated anonymously. Believed to have belonged to Amos Kirkland.

"The Kirkland family certainly left their mark on Meadowood," I murmured, brushing my fingers lightly over the edge. The wood felt cool and smooth under my fingertips. The patina polished to a warm glow. One of the lower drawers was slightly ajar, catching my attention. Hmm, that doesn't look right. Maybe it just needs a nudge to fix it.

I glanced around. No one was watching.

Carefully, I tugged on the knob, intending to straighten the drawer. It slid open with a creak, revealing an empty velvet-lined interior. I crouched down to inspect it closer. Something didn't sit right. The drawer seemed too shallow.

Reaching in, I pressed my fingers against the back panel. It gave, just a bit. My curiosity was really piqued. I had to explore more.

I fumbled around the edges until my fingers caught a tiny notch under the knob. When I pressed it, a small click sounded, and a false back popped loose, revealing a narrow hidden compartment.

Heart racing, my breath caught in my throat as my fingers delved into the tiny space. Inside was a folded piece of parchment, yellowed with age.

"Merry!" Colleen called from behind. Startled, I jerked upward, nearly hitting my head on the edge of the desk. As I rose from my stooped position, I clutched the paper and slipped it into my bag. I quickly slid the drawer shut and stepped away.

"Over here," I said, trying to sound casual. She joined me with her husband Ron, who carried their glasses of cider.

"This place is amazing," Colleen said, eyes wide. "Did you see the butter churn with initials carved into it? That was from the first homestead on Cedar Ridge."

"I was just admiring this desk," I said with a smile, but my heart was pounding.

"Impressive. I see it's from the Kirkland estate," Colleen mentioned as she ran her hand lightly over the smooth finish.

We strolled toward one of the other rooms.

A nameplate at the entrance to the room announced the Society of Free Men. I entered the room to examine the artifacts that Colleen and I knew personally from one of our past escapades. I turned to tap Colleen on the shoulder.

"Remember these?" I asked.

"How can I forget? You had me cowering in a closet fearful of being caught any minute," Colleen laughed.

A purple satin banner proclaiming the Society of Free Men, written in Latin, hung above a long, narrow table covered in a gold brocade cloth. A unique set of triple candleholders, a Trikirion, was placed on each end of the table. A huge leather-bound book, its gold-leaf lettering worn smooth on both spine and cover, lay in a place of honor on the center of the table. The large placard hanging next to the display explained the history of the organization. Founded in 1810 by the white landowners of the region, it was a pact to protect each other and to help neighbors against all intruders. The secret society had remained in existence until the bicentennial of Meadowood, when it was finally disbanded last year.

"Yeah, but it all turned out okay," I said as I fingered the silver candelabra.

As I turned around, I bumped into another visitor examining the objects. "Excuse me," I said then stumbled over my own feet as I recognized Kevin Wyatt. His eyes widened at the same time.

"We meet again. How ironic I run into you at the display of the S.O.F.M.," Wyatt sneered.

"I didn't know you were back."

"No law against a person returning to their former home."

"No. I guess not. See you around," I said, shifting my gaze to my waiting friends.

We left and strolled through the remaining space. Thoughts swirled in my mind. How weird to run into Kevin Wyatt, and here of all places after the disgraced banker and president of the secret society had fled town. Shaking my head to clear it, I focused on the paper hidden in my purse. My fingers itched to unfold it and learn its secrets.

Back near the refreshment table, I made an excuse to visit the restroom, then ducked into a quiet hallway, and carefully unfolded the parchment.

The writing was in old-fashioned script, faint and hard to read. I squinted to make out the message: *The key to the Iron Pledge lies beneath the silent bell. Trust not the steward in shadow. Signed - A.K.*

I stared at it. What on earth?

I folded it back up and hid it in my purse again.

Returning to the exhibit, my gaze kept drifting to Carl Bradley, who was deep in conversation with Trixie Jones. She seemed to press him for an answer. If I knew Trixie, she had discovered something in our director's past and was probing for details.

Bradley's voice raised angrily. "You print that nonsense and I'll sue you for libel."

People around him stopped talking and stared at his outburst. Bradley immediately lowered his voice and rearranged the expression on his face. He nodded politely and then stepped away from the reporter. I stood nearby, watching. His eyes met mine, and something in his expression changed. Tense. Guarded.

Had he seen me at the desk? Did he guess I had found the secret message? I never had what is called a poker face; mine betrayed me with my thoughts and feelings guiltily displayed. I worried the director suspected I had something to hide.

Doug came up beside me, catching the direction of my gaze. "What was that all about?" He gestured toward Trixie and the director's retreating back.

"Not sure," I said, worried my secrets showed. "I don't think I care for our new director."

Trixie sidled over, her voice low. "I've got the scoop on our new director. Wait until I tell you ... hey, did you find something in there? I noticed you examining that desk. What gives?"

I gave her a sharp look. "Keep your voice down."

She smirked. "I've seen that look on your face before. C'mon. I want to know what you know. You found something, didn't you?"

"I'll tell you later. Jeez Louise, can you just keep quiet for right now?"

My mind spun. Who was A.K.? What was the *iron pledge*? And why warn against a steward in shadow? That sounded like something out of a spy novel.

The celebration continued around us, with recorded music playing softly in the background. Guests mingled, sipped apple cider, and nibbled Martha's miniature strawberry tarts. But I couldn't shake the chill that had settled over me that had nothing to do with the brisk October air.

There were secrets in that museum, and not all of them involved historic artifacts.

Chapter Six

Masquerade

A chill ran down my spine, like a bad premonition. I should've known something was off the moment the Phantom of the Opera showed up. My past dealings with a phantom at Halloween had ended in trouble, causing me to worry this one might end the same.

Doug and I stood near the speakeasy-style bar. He looked dashing in his yellow trench coat and fedora hat as Dick Tracy, while I'd done my best with a 1940s hair bob and a blue pencil skirt to channel Tracy's faithful Tess Trueheart. I had a red clutch tucked under one arm and a plastic toy pistol tucked into my belt, just for flair. Doug's sheriff's badge was hidden tonight, replaced with a detective's scowl and a bit too much gel in his hair. Every once in a while, Doug made a point of checking his special two-way wrist radio, even if it was only his Fitbit smartwatch. It looked just like Tracy's watch. I laughed at his attempt to stay in character.

"Merry, this is incredible. We're having a huge turnout," Colleen said, sweeping up beside me in her emerald green satin gown, a martini glass perched between her fingers. She and her husband Ron had nailed the glamorous Nick and Nora Charles look—him in a tuxedo and pencil mustache, her with a long string of pearls and sly eyes. "Whoever thought of using the old church as a banquet hall should win an award. When my team worked on adding the flowers and decorations, I still had my doubts whether this building would make a good venue. But just look ... it's fabulous. Everyone is having a great time. We should collect an enormous pot of money from party ticket sales for the food drive."

"Leave it to Aunt Fran," I said, nodding toward the mayor, who was gliding across the floor in a sea of cream silk, looking every bit the grand dame as Edith Vanderbilt. Diamonds sparkled on her gloves and at her throat. "She envisioned the museum and the event venue working together. Though she had to fight the council tooth and nail for that renovation budget."

"Well, it's great. I don't know what's more fun," Colleen added with a grin, "the band, the costumes, or that Chuck Thompson just tried to lasso the cheese tray."

"You're kidding!" I exclaimed as I spotted Chuck.

"Yee-ha!" shouted Chuck, dressed as cowboy Roy Rodgers in a black shirt and pants with a pearl-handled Colt 45 riding in a silver-trimmed gun holster on his hips. Anna sidled up to him in her tan buckskin dress adorned with colorful beads across the bodice. Long cowhide fringe hung from her wrists and hemline, while a white Stetson hat perched on her head. I would have known them anywhere despite the half masks they wore.

"Giddy-up!" Anna called out then hooted with laughter.

Jeez Louise, had my friends indulged in too much moonshine? I wondered as I stared at their antics. Oh yeah, she was going to have a pounding hangover tomorrow.

Anna waved playfully as she and Chuck moseyed over to the buffet table.

I laughed at the pair then turned in time to see our fire chief in full Mountie regalia, his wide hat nearly knocking over a stack of carved pumpkins. His wife Carol, dressed as a pouty Nell, fluttered after him with mock dismay, her corset barely holding up under the strain of good intentions and two glasses of sangria.

The best part of this party was the people-watching. Everyone's costumes showed an amazing amount of thought and creativity. I don't think I saw any duplicates. Taking out my cell phone, I snapped photos of the many stunning characters.

After viewing Teresa with her bright hair this morning, I was curious how she would dress tonight. But she made use of that hair color by arriving as little Orphan Annie. Her brother Alvin came as Johnny Appleseed with a backpack slung over his shoulder filled with green apples and a battered ball cap worn backwards on his head. I smiled at the sight of him. Only Alvin could have thought to dress as Johnny Appleseed, John Chapman, the pioneer nurseryman who planted trees grown from apple seeds in Ohio and the western territories of colonial America.

Outside, a full moon peeked over the old bell tower behind the church. A line of carved jack-o'-lanterns flickered along the stone walkway that connected the museum to the church. The air smelled of dry leaves, cloves, and pumpkin spice, with the faint tang of apples. Mums in big pots filled the corners of the dance hall: gold, bronze, white. Glorious riots of autumn color. Cornstalks rustled against the stone walls, and every few minutes the crisp wind blowing through the open doorway threatened to steal someone's feathered headpiece or ruffle satin skirts.

A jazz trio played near the front, where the altar used to be. The buffet stretched the length of the east wall, offering a smorgasbord of fall favorites: platters of roasted butternut squash, baked apples sprinkled with cinnamon, tiny meatballs in a brown sugar glaze, pulled barbecue pork, and hot apple cider laced with bourbon. A second buffet table was laden with every kind of baked goods to satisfy the biggest sweet tooth. The bar was rigged like a hidden speakeasy; you had to knock and tell the greeter, "Joe sent me" before they'd grin and usher you in past the velvet rope. It was pure fun.

The ambiance felt light and playful. Guests laughed and joked, acting out their costumed characters.

But then Carl Bradley walked in. Pompous ... an outsider among the Meadowood citizens enjoying themselves here tonight.

For one thing, he was late and unapologetic. And for another, he dressed in a black cape and white mask that covered half his face ... committed to the Phantom image right down to the silver-tipped cane and melodramatic scowl. He stalked past guests without so much as a nod. The music seemed to falter when he entered, as if even the band had noticed the shift in mood.

Doug leaned over and whispered, "That guy acts like he's got a stick up his butt. Think he knows this is supposed to be a party?"

"I'm not sure Carl Bradley knows what fun is," I replied.

I watched as my Aunt Fran tried to get his attention, but he turned away from the mayor, leaving her to stand and gape after him.

Keeping an eye on him, I saw him make his way toward the bar, demanding a drink of whiskey. None other than Trixie Jones — dressed like a flapper straight out of *Chicago*, complete with sequins and a feathered headband —perched on a barstool, swirling her wine like a threat.

Their exchange started quietly, all tight smiles and clipped words. But it didn't stay polite for long. Trixie could be a force to be reckoned with.

"I told you to back off," Bradley hissed loud enough for me—and half the room—to hear. "One more insinuation like that, or a false story printed in that little rag of yours, could cause that newspaper to go up in flames."

Trixie stood. "Are you threatening me, *director*? I'm not the only one wondering about who you really are and where you came from before Fairview College. What are you hiding? Who are you, really?"

Carl's eyes glittered like twin coals. "Leave me alone. You have no idea what you're digging into. Back off or you'll be sorry."

That's when Trixie, with all the flair of a woman who'd seen one too many black-and-white films, tossed the contents of her wine glass straight into Carl's masked face.

Gasps rippled across the room. Carl sputtered, swore, then stormed out the side door toward the museum, his cape billowing like some kind of gothic bat. Trixie turned on her heel and stalked toward the dance floor, snatching another glass of wine from a passing tray with a muttered, "Power of the press."

I moved toward her, intending to intervene or defuse whatever this was turning into, but Doug gently caught my wrist.

"Let them both cool down," he said. "No reason to start another scene. I'll take care of it if it grows into something more."

Georgia followed Trixie across the room and pulled on her arm, spinning her around, causing her drink to slosh over the glass rim.

"What is wrong with you? Why are you attacking that dear man?" Georgia demanded.

"Are you nuts? Let go of my arm. I'm just reporting the truth about that guy." Trixie pulled free of the domineering woman and walked away from her.

The party carried on, though quieter now. People whispered. The town gossips speculated. Eyes followed Trixie like she'd grown horns. But soon the band picked up again, someone started a Charleston, and people laughed and giggled as they recreated the lively thirties' dance steps. Champagne flowed and townsfolks celebrated. The music switched up to Glenn Miller and Benny Goodman hits while the dancing continued under the old church rafters and twinkle lights.

"How about a twirl on the dance floor?" Doug whispered in my ear.

"Love to. Thought you'd never ask," I replied as I stepped into his arms and we moved among the dancers.

We ate and sipped champagne, delighting in the company of our friends and the merriment of the party. Everything was perfect ... almost.

It was close to midnight when a scream rent the night.

Pushing through the crowd, we rushed toward the sound in the dark night. Doug ran ahead of me, visible in his bright yellow trench coat, as we crossed the wide grassy yard that separated the church-turned-ballroom from the newly christened Meadowood History Museum.

A woman stood to one side, pointing to the ground. She covered her face with her hands, then turned away from the sight.

Alvin Maxwell lay crumpled at the base of the brick steps leading up to the museum's grand doors, his life force drained. Apples lay strewn along the path from his tossed backpack.

A wide gash split his scalp. Congealed blood filled his hair and trickled down his temple, pooling in the grass and soaking into the dry leaves scattered across the walkway. A harsh metallic scent filled the air.

Doug dropped to one knee next to the body, checking for a pulse. His face was grim when he stood.

"He's dead."

I stood frozen, staring at the body beneath the autumn moon, surrounded by cracked pumpkins and with the scent of cold cider still on the wind. Why Alvin? Who would kill this man?

Teresa screamed, rushed forward, and kneeled next to her brother. Her mascara smudged into black streaks as tears streamed down her face at the senseless killing of such a sweet, gentle man.

My eyes searched the ground near him. I gasped as I spotted a silver-tipped cane, covered in blood, plastered with dried leaves under a bush.

The party was over. But the mystery had just begun.

Chapter Seven

Alvin's Secret

The festive glow of lanterns flickered behind Sheriff Gardner as he stood over the body of Alvin Maxwell. The music inside the old church-turned-dance-hall had gone silent, replaced by murmurs, the occasional gasp, and the scraping of heels against wood as guests peered from the doorway, hushed and pale.

Doug's hand instinctively went to the radio normally clipped to his belt — missing. He was in costume tonight, but beneath the Dick Tracy hat and yellow coat, he was still Meadowood's sheriff.

"Give me your cell phone," Doug demanded of Merry. She opened her clutch purse and pulled out the phone.

He rapidly dialed the number for the sheriff's office.

"This is Gardner," he said as soon as the deputy answered. "We've got a 10-66. Victim confirmed deceased. Send EMT and backup to the museum entrance on East Walnut. Secure perimeter."

He crouched low, inspecting the young man's body with practiced calm. Alvin Maxwell's farmer overalls were torn at the shoulder and soaked in blood. A deep head wound just above the left ear suggested the likely cause of death.

Doug's jaw tightened. He'd known the Maxwells for years—Teresa ran the hair salon and had cut his boys' hair since they were toddlers. Alvin was quiet, sweet-natured, and a bit of a history buff like Merry. He didn't belong within a scene like this.

Doug rose and turned to one of his deputies, who had just arrived. "Rope off this entire section of the lawn. I want photos, bagged evidence, and footprints logged. Handle that silver-tipped cane with care." He pointed to the long black walking cane protruding from the boxwood shrub. "We'll need to check security footage from both the church building and the museum."

He looked toward the cluster of guests gathered near the stone path, still in their elaborate costumes, eyes wide, faces drained of color beneath wigs and powdered makeup. The masquerade had turned into a horror show.

Doctor Stone, Meadowood's local town physician and acting coroner, had arrived to examine the body. He stood slowly and snapped his black bag shut.

"What do you think, Doc?" asked Doug.

"Death by blunt force trauma, definitely. Irregular shaped wound. Small fragments of a reddish stone, possibly brick, in the scalp. I'll know better when I can examine him in better light."

"Thanks Doc."

The EMTs took Alvin's body away, while the deputies fully secured the crime scene .

Doug pulled his notebook from his coat pocket and handed back Merry's cell phone. Time to get to work.

Thirty Minutes Later:

Weary guests had been ushered back inside the church hall,

where the band had packed up and volunteers had broken down the buffet table. Deputy Tony Dalton questioned the guests, slowly making his way from person to person in the hall. Doug paced the perimeter of the cordoned-off yard, mentally retracing Alvin's steps. The area was littered with brittle leaves, a few crushed mums, and a jagged broken brick lying near the museum's staircase and foundation, apparently overlooked during the renovation work. He stooped to examine it closer.

Dalton approached with a clipboard. "We confirmed Alvin was last seen heading toward the museum just after the clash between Bradley and Trixie Jones. Several guests saw him go in that direction alone. No one saw him come back."

"Did anyone see Carl Bradley leave?" Doug asked, already guessing the answer.

Dalton shook his head. "He hasn't been seen since he stormed out after the wine incident. We searched the museum, basement, and office ... he's not there. His car is still in the lot, though."

Doug nodded grimly. "Issue a BOLO for Carl Bradley. If he's hiding, I want eyes on every exit road in the county. And Tony, bag that broken brick, looks like it has blood on it."

Doug stepped back into the church, where the flickering candlelight now seemed somber rather than celebratory. The cornstalks and orange twinkle lights no longer added warmth—just a shadowy hush to the wide space that only an hour ago was alive with laughter and jazz music.

He found Trixie seated near the old pulpit, wrapped in a borrowed shawl. Her makeup had smudged from crying ... or from being questioned repeatedly by police officers and town gossips.

"Trixie," Doug said as he approached, voice steady.

Her eyes flashed, defensive. "Don't even start. I had nothing to do with this."

"I didn't say you did." He sank into a chair beside her and

lowered his voice. "But you argued with Bradley in front of fifty people. Then both Bradley and Alvin left and Alvin comes up dead. What can you tell me?"

"I didn't even talk to Alvin tonight. I didn't know he was involved or would chase after Bradley," she snapped.

Doug frowned. "Involved in what?"

Trixie looked at him, lips pressed tight.

He waited.

"You know I can't tell you that, Sheriff," she said and crossed her arms, giving Doug a defiant glare.

"Well if your source was Alvin Maxwell, he's dead. Now tell me what you know."

"I've been following a paper trail," she finally whispered. "Alvin helped carry boxes of records and things from storage when the museum displays were being set up. He was one of the volunteers. Alvin found something in the museum archives — something about property deeds dating from the town's founding. He showed them to the new director, but Bradley wanted them buried. Teresa told me her brother was scared to go public. Alvin didn't trust Bradley."

Doug's brows lifted. "Forged deeds?"

"Yes. Some old documents from the 1820s. Land ownership disputes involving the founding families — Maxwell, Johnson, even the old Kirkland estate. Alvin believed Bradley might have hidden evidence of those original claims and was creating forged documents. He told me Bradley was looking for a vault or records room that hadn't been accessed yet. Somewhere under the bell tower, or the chapel maybe."

Doug rubbed a hand across his chin. "Where are those documents now? Are you certain Bradley was involved?"

Trixie leaned closer. "I dunno. That's what Alvin was trying to prove. He said Bradley was plotting to rewrite history to favor new investors. If Alvin was right, the Maxwells, and other families still have claims to some of the land around the town square."

"And now Alvin's dead," Doug muttered.

A chill crawled down his spine.

Storm clouds obscured the moon, casting the inky night into a sinister scene. Exhausted party-goers straggled out of the church and made their way home. Their fun, gay evening had shattered into a night of sorrow and horror. In a couple of hours, dawn would lighten the sky on a new day, but not for Alvin Maxwell.

Fran wrapped her fur stole tighter around her shoulders as she left the warmth of the ballroom. The thrill of the museum opening and the party celebration faded into an illusory dream after the harsh reality of a citizen's death. One of her citizens. The mayor swallowed a sob as she thought of the loss of that innocent man and the failure of her pet project, forever marred now in tragedy.

"Goodnight, Aunt Fran," Merry called as she waited by her car. Merry lifted a hand to wave weakly. She needed her bed and sleep. Sleep to dull her mind and wake up to find this had all been a nightmare.

Doug stood alone near the front steps of the museum, staring at the worn path between the bell tower and the museum door. His eyes followed the shadows to the side entrance, where Carl Bradley had disappeared.

Doug didn't believe in coincidence—not in a small town like Meadowood.

Alvin Maxwell had uncovered something he wasn't supposed to.

Carl Bradley had motive, means, and now he was missing.

Doug straightened, scanned the museum windows again, and said privately to his deputy, "Post a guard. Nobody goes into the museum and no one is allowed to go snooping behind the church or on the grounds."

"Got it Sheriff. Good night."

"Is it?"

Doug and Merry climbed into their car and drove home in silence. The morning would be upon them all too soon, and with it more questions than they had answers.

Chapter Eight

Mysterious Message

I t was a somber morning in the A&M Tea shop as Anna and I poured steaming pots of tea and served petite sandwiches, delicious scones, and muffins. Even our customers seemed quieter.

"What time did you and Doug finally get home?" asked Anna as she handed me a pot of brewed Earl Grey.

"Not until after two in the morning. I still can't believe what happened," I said as I carried the pot into the dining room and served two ladies I recognized from last week's church tour.

The bell over the door jangled, grating on my nerves and lack of sleep. Trixie hurried into the shop holding a folded newspaper that I suspected was the morning edition. I motioned for her to follow me into the kitchen.

"Read this," Trixie said as she shoved the paper at me.

I unfolded the newsprint. Glaring headlines in bold lettering screamed MURDER. I quickly scanned the news article, where Trixie described the grand opening of the Meadowood museum followed by the celebration and masquerade party where Alvin Maxwell was found bludgeoned to death. She mentioned the new director, Dr. Carl Bradley, and his suspicious credentials and went so far as to question his credibility and potential link to the murder. I shot her a look as I read the accusations.

"You are bordering on libel, you know. He could claim defamation of character with some of the charges you're laying on him. Aren't you worried he will sue you?" I asked.

I handed the paper to Anna since she was straining her neck to read over my shoulder. Minutes later, Anna had the same reaction. "Honey child, you're just asking for trouble. Can you prove any of these claims?"

"Most. Merry, you tried researching Bradley's background. What did you find? The man doesn't exist before his time at Fairview. Don't tell me that's not suspicious."

"You won't get any argument from me on that point. I'd like to know where he took off to last night. We found his cane near Alvin's body. It had blood on the tip. If he's innocent, why did he run off?"

"I tell you, things just don't add up. Alvin tried to talk to me about what he'd found at the museum, but he wasn't making any sense."

"So are you publishing the paper today with that story on the front page?" Anna asked.

"Yes. The public has the right to know about the illustrious museum director our town council hired."

"Come around after two o'clock when we can talk. I've got something to show you," I told Trixie.

"I knew it! You found something at the museum. I saw you snooping around in that antique desk. That's it, isn't it?" Trixie said excitedly, her voice rising.

"Shush! Someone will hear you." I warned as I waved my hands in front of her.

"All right. I'll be back," Trixie said and skipped out of the shop.

Anna looked over at me and laughed. "That gal is a whirlwind of activity. Just hope it doesn't get her in trouble."

I locked the door after the last customer left, and Trixie slipped in. Anna had a table set up for us toward the back of the shop. She sat down and stretched out her legs.

"Ah, that feels good. I think all the activity from yesterday is catching up to me. I'm not as young as I used to be, girls."

I grabbed my purse from the coat hook in the kitchen and carried it to the table. Anna and Trixie looked at me expectantly.

"Okay. You're right. Yesterday when I was in the museum, I was admiring an antique desk from the Kirkland family. A small bottom drawer sat crooked so I pulled it out to straighten it, but when I did, I noticed the inside didn't quite look correct. I felt around and my fingers touched a clasp that made the bottom drop and I found a piece of rolled up parchment."

"What was written on it?" asked Anna. She poured hot tea for the three of us. I waited until she was done before spreading out the fragile paper on the tabletop.

"Be careful. This paper is really old. What do you think of this?" I asked in a low voice, afraid to speak in more than a whisper.

"The key to the Iron Pledge lies beneath the silent bell. Trust not the steward in shadow. — A.K."

"What iron pledge? Who is the steward in shadow? This sounds like some secret spy message. Hey, do you think it involved the Society of Free Men? They probably went into this encrypted stuff," Trixie voiced her thoughts out loud, echoing my own.

"I was thinking the same thing. The time frame fits. The desk is from the same period when the S.O.F.M. organized. Maybe the iron pledge refers to their secret pact to protect the families and their lands. I don't know but I'd like to learn more."

"And the silent bell? Could that be the old bell tower next to the Methodist church we were in last night? I did some research on the history of those buildings before writing my article on the museum and found the church was original to the town ... built in 1824," Trixie explained.

"Wow, I knew it was old but I didn't realize it went back that far. It's been vacant for close to fifteen years ever since the congregation build their new church structure over on Meadow Lane. The new Methodist church and Bible school stretches across most of that hillside. It's a beautiful location," I said.

"Yeah, um, that's all well and good but what about this warning ... this message? Who is the steward not to be trusted? What is that supposed to mean?" Trixie asked. Her reporter skepticism rising to the surface.

"Maybe we need to do some digging around. Are you game?" I asked. My eyes met Trixie's.

"Count me in. What about you, Anna? Are you going to join our search for the silent bell?" asked Trixie with a wink to me.

"I think I'll sit this one out, girls. But you best let me know when you start this nonsense in case I have to enlist help to rescue you both," Anna said.

I laughed. "You make us sound like we're going on a search for hidden treasure like *Indiana Jones*. What could go wrong?"

"Humph! Famous last words," Anna said with a snort.

"I've got to get out the newspaper right now. Let's meet in the morning at the church. I'll bring everything I printed off in my research plus notes from what Alvin told me," Trixie said.

"All right. See you tomorrow. I'm going to check in on Aunt Fran and see how's she's holding up after last night."

Anna and I left the tea shop. She drove toward home, and I walked the two blocks to Frannie's Frocks.

Corn stalks and a collection of pumpkins were arranged around pots of golden mums by the entrance to the dress shop. Betty worked behind the register as I entered the store. Displays of soft knit sweaters and pullover tops in fall colors were arranged near the front of the store. Coordinating corduroy or wool trousers hung near them. I walked past the attractive displays and found my aunt in the back stockroom.

She glanced up as I approached, pausing with the price tags and sale stickers she'd been attaching to a pile of new shirts. Her eyes were red and showed signs of crying.

I wrapped my arms around her, and we clung to each other silently. "I'm sorry," I said.

"What for? You did nothing."

"I know. I just mean I'm sorry your dream had to be so cruelly broken."

The front door slammed. The loud commotion brought Fran and me out of the back to witness Betty trying to calm a disturbed Teresa Maxwell.

"You're the reason my sweet Alvin is dead!" screamed Teresa, pointing her finger at Fran and waving her arms around wildly. "You brought that man into our town! It's your fault."

"Who?"

"That ... that so called history professor, Bradley. He did this. You know he did."

The accusation was unfair, but I saw my aunt crushed by Teresa's words. She had been blaming herself for Alvin's death, now this ...

"You don't mean that," I said to Teresa.

"It's true. I do feel responsible," Fran said in a soft voice.

"Stop it, both of you. Teresa, we're all sorry for your loss. Alvin was a fine man. You know Doug will do everything he can to find his killer. You're hurting. I understand, but it's not anyone's fault except the killer's," I spoke softly and tried to put my arms around my friend and offer her support.

Teresa sobbed and collapsed onto the floor. Fran and I both rushed to help her to her feet and guided her into the back, offering Teresa a chair. Fran fixed her a cup of coffee while I stood next to Teresa, rubbing her back and speaking softly to her. Her grief filled the room like a palpable wall of emotion.

"We'll find who did this," Fran stated.

"Who else could it be except Bradley? He threatened my brother. Alvin told me and now he's dead," Teresa sobbed again with a fresh onslaught of tears.

It was an hour before we could calm the distraught woman. Fran drove Teresa home and left poor Betty to close up the dress shop while I walked back to my own vehicle parked behind the tea shop. It had been a long and exhausting day.

The telephone ringing woke me from a sound sleep. Doug roused and picked up the phone, any trace of grogginess gone from his voice as he questioned the caller.

"Are you in a safe place? Do you still hear any noise downstairs? I'll be right there."

"What is it? Who called?" I asked, sitting up in bed. I watched my husband hastily drag on a pair of pants and a shirt.

"Trixie. She thinks someone has broken into the newspaper office. They might still be there."

"Oh my goodness! Is she all right? I'm coming with you," I declared, jumping out of bed, but he wasn't waiting.

Doug dashed out of the bedroom and ran down the stairs. I heard the back door open and close, then his car sped away into the night before I had a chance to move.

After dressing, I went downstairs and started a pot of coffee while I waited anxiously to hear what had happened to Trixie. Finally, over an hour later, Doug phoned.

"Trixie is fine. Her shop was vandalized. No actual damage but she's got a mess to clean up. Guy was gone by the time I got there."

"How did he get in? Was anything stolen?" I asked Doug as I poured myself a second mug of coffee.

"It looks like someone jimmied the front door and split the door frame. Trixie will have to get that fixed. She was still sorting through her files when I left, so I don't know if anything was taken yet. I'd say yesterday's news story ruffled some feathers."

"You know what that means. Only one person would have been upset by yesterday's story ... Carl Bradley. Have you found him yet?" I asked.

"My deputies are still looking for the director. I'll be home in a little while. I've got to write up the report on this break-in. Don't go running off half-cocked. Okay? I know you've become invested in this thing."

"I won't," I promised with my fingers crossed behind my back.

Chapter Nine

Vandals

*S*unday morning, Colleen should be home, I thought to myself as I grabbed my cell phone. I dialed my friend; relieved when she answered after the second ring.

"Hey, are you busy today?" I asked.

"Why?" Colleen replied with a hint of trepidation. I heard it in her voice.

"Nothing like what you're thinking. Relax. Trixie's newspaper office got broken into earlier today. I wanted to go see her and I thought you might want to join me."

"Oh. Now I feel guilty for mistrusting you. Sure, I can stop over. I've got to do a load of laundry first; let me throw that in the machine and I can step out," Colleen said.

"Oh, that reminds me ... I've got a load of towels and napkins in the dryer for the shop. I better get them folded. See you at Trixie's in about thirty minutes. Okay?"

"Sounds good."

. . .

Rain pelted my windshield as I drove to Trixie's building, thankful to find a parking place along the empty street. Cold fall temperatures dropped even lower as the rain continued and the morning dragged on.

I knocked on the door, huddled under my umbrella, and waited on Trixie to let me in. Colleen rushed up to me just as Trixie unlocked the door. We both hurried into the disheveled office, grateful for the warmth.

"Gosh, what a mess," Colleen exclaimed as she looked around.

Vandals had turned over equipment; copy machines spilled black powdery toner onto the floor. A ream of copy paper lay scattered about the room like a pile of windblown leaves. File cabinet drawers were pulled open and folders rifled.

"Can you tell if anything is missing? Do you think whoever did this was looking for information or just wanted to cause trouble?" I asked.

"Nothing is missing that I can tell. Mostly I think somebody just wanted to make a statement and disrupt the paper. If he thinks this will stop me, he's got another think coming. A stack of blank paper doesn't make the newspaper ... it's the data and stories saved on my computer in the cloud and inside my brain. He couldn't get past my encrypted password and laptop login, unless he chopped off my thumb ... takes my thumb print to log onto my computer security," Trixie explained.

"Jeez Louise, you really take this security stuff seriously," I said.

"Uh-huh, and for good reason."

"What can we do to help?" Colleen asked.

Trixie turned in a circle as she looked around the small office. "Colleen, if you could put my files back in order that would help. Merry, give me a hand setting up these copy machines and sweeping up the paper and toner from the floor. I think that's the worse of it."

"Sure. Where can we hang our coats and handbags? Let's get started," I said, rolling up my sleeves and grabbing a broom.

We silently worked side by side, putting the news office back to rights. As we finished scooping up the last of the toner mess, Trixie turned to me.

"Thought we were going to search for the silent bell today?"

Colleen shot me a look as she closed the file drawer. "Silent bell? What's going on?" She glanced between Trixie and me.

"I, uh, found a message hidden in a drawer of that antique desk in the museum." Digging the parchment paper from my purse, I handed it to Colleen. "Read this."

Colleen held the paper and read out loud, *"The key to the Iron Pledge lies beneath the silent bell. Trust not the steward in shadow. – A.K.* Who's A.K.? You said you found this in that desk, the one we were admiring? Do I want to know how you simply found a piece of paper?" She stood with her hands on her hips, waving the paper at me.

"That's not important. We think the *iron pledge* refers to the Society of Free Men and maybe the silent bell is inside the old bell tower of the Methodist church."

"Oh no, not them again. Didn't you cause enough trouble the last time we got mixed up with the S.O.F.M.? I saw Kevin Wyatt at the museum too, " Colleen asked in a tight voice.

I shot her a look pleading for her understanding. Sometimes, Colleen was just too uptight and couldn't see the bigger picture.

"We were planning on hunting for the bell, but then Trixie got vandalized. Besides, I've been thinking about it. I've got some doubts," I said.

"Doubts? What are you talking about?" asked Trixie.

"Well, it's just that finding the bell mentioned in this message at the church bell tower seems too easy. If this so-called silent bell was hidden two hundred years ago, don't you think it would be some place less obvious? I mean, c'mon, a bell tower? If it was there, someone would have found it ages ago," I argued.

"Hmm, you've got a point. But why can't it be that simple? I still think we should look. Might have to wait until the rain stops though," Trixie said.

Colleen looked back and forth at the two of us like we were crazy. I guess we sounded crazy talking about hunting for a lost bell like it represented some archaeological treasure.

Seeking to assuage my best friend's annoyance with me, I suggested a more agreeable outing.

"Martha's bakery is still open. How about we drop in for a hot bowl of soup and one of her luncheon pastries? I think a buttery croissant is calling my name," I said with a chuckle.

"Guess there's nothing more we can do here. Hot soup sounds tasty on a miserable day like today," Colleen agreed reluctantly.

"Let's take my car. It's right out front," I said as we all bundled up and grabbed umbrellas.

Martha waved a welcoming hand as we approached the bakery door. The bakery's warmth enveloped us as we entered; our nostrils filled with heady scents of cinnamon and caramel, freshly baked yeast breads, and the tang of butternut squash soup simmering on the stove.

"Are we too late for lunch?" I asked, closing my umbrella and propping it by the door.

"No, of course not. I was considering closing early because of the weather, but you're more than welcome. It's good to see all of you. What can I get you?" asked Martha.

"I'll have a bowl of that delicious smelling soup and a croissant," I said. "Mmm, maybe one of those apple Danish for dessert."

"Coming right up. Hey Trixie, what was all the commotion about down at your end of the street? I'm usually the only one awake in the wee hours of the morning," Martha said.

"My newspaper office got broken into and vandalized," Trixie replied. "We've got it cleaned up now." She brushed raindrops off her coat and then said, "Bring me the same as Merry, thanks."

"Oh goodness! I'm sorry to hear you had trouble."

Colleen ordered the same, then Martha left us to get comfortable at a table while she got busy serving up bowls of the hot soup in the kitchen. Balancing a heavy tray loaded with bowls and plates, Martha set it down on an empty table, then turned to serve us.

"Looks like we have the place to ourselves. Guess everyone came in early to get their Sunday morning treats. Sit down and join us, Martha," I said.

"I suppose I can. Doesn't look like any more customers will venture out on such a soggy day."

Martha went back to pour herself a bowl of the creamy butternut squash soup and then slipped into a chair at our table.

"Mmm, this soup is so tasty. Perfect choice for this time of the year," Colleen commented.

"Has anyone spoken to poor Teresa since Friday night?" Martha asked.

"Yeah. Aunt Fran and I spoke to her late Saturday. She was pretty upset about Alvin, even blamed Fran for bringing Carl Bradley to town. Naturally she suspects Bradley of killing Alvin," I said as I finished my bowl of soup.

"Oh no!" Martha said, her hands covering her mouth.

"Do we know for a fact that Bradley killed Alvin?" asked Colleen, ever the logical member of our group.

"Well, Doug found his cane near the body with blood on the tip. Plus, the man is missing. If he's innocent, why is he hiding?" I asked.

"I'd bet that he was the person who broke into my office, too. My article really enraged him; he even threatened me over the phone," Trixie said.

"Does Doug know that? You never said he called you. When was this?" I asked. My mind considered this new information. Why would Bradley phone Trixie first and then vandalize her office later?

"I don't know. I think I told him. Maybe. With everything happening at the party and then later, I'm not sure now."

"Let's suppose that it wasn't Bradley who wrecked your office; who else might have a beef with you or the paper?" I asked.

"I have no idea," Trixie said in a low voice as her brow wrinkled. She bit her lower lip and stared into the gloomy wet day.

The plate glass shop window reflected our worried faces as rivulets of rainwater slid down the glass like Meadowood tears shed for its lost citizen.

Chapter Ten

Silent Bell

Trixie and I stood beneath the leaning bell tower of the old chapel. After the morning's heavy rain, the place smelled of damp stone and aged cedar, and the air carried a faint metallic tang that reminded me of forgotten cellars and storm-battered barns. Rainwater dripped from the upper beams.

"I can't believe you convinced me to do this. Usually I'm the one that gets blamed for leading others astray."

"Merry, are you sure this is the one?" Trixie asked, tugging her jacket tighter against the afternoon chill.

"No. Not really," I said, pointing up toward the rotted wooden slats and rusted iron bell. "This church bell has been silent for nearly a century. I just don't know if it's the same one described on the parchment."

We climbed the narrow wooden spiral stairs of the tower, each wet step slippery and groaning beneath our weight. Dust and cobwebs clung to the railing. Near the platform where the bell hung crooked, I spotted it ... a faint carving on a crossbeam.

"Look there," I whispered.

A weathered insignia, almost obscured by grime, was carved into the wood. It looked like a stylized triangle wrapped in vines, with a tiny hammer at its base.

"What does it mean?" Trixie asked. She snapped several photos of the beam and the carved insignia.

"Not sure. I don't see anything else around the bell. Obviously, we can't climb any higher; maybe we need to look lower. Let's see if there's a basement or a space connecting the tower with the church," I said as I carefully turned to maneuver the descending rickety staircase.

"Wouldn't the contractors have found something when they updated the church?" Trixie asked.

"I don't think they touched the lower floor, just the main upper rooms."

Trixie followed me to the base of the stairs. The overcast sky dulled the meager amount of late afternoon light filtering into the tower. I patted my coat pocket, grateful for the flashlight I'd brought on this crazy search. Our hands felt along the walls of the tower looking for a hidden door or another carving that might lead the way. Hopeless.

Then Trixie kneeled beside a section of warped wood on the floor and frowned. "Something's off with the seam lines down here. And what's this?"

I joined her. A rusted iron ring, buried in dirt and dried leaves, was bolted into the floor. We exchanged a look.

"Help me pull."

Together we gripped the ring and tugged; the wood groaned with resistance. Finally, with a loud crack and a puff of dust, the panel came loose. The effort knocked both of us onto our rumps. Another hinged wooden slab was revealed beneath.

Douglas Gardner left the sheriff's office and headed over to his wife's tea shop. He hadn't talked to her all day, and now he couldn't dismiss a funny feeling he had in the pit of his stomach. A feeling he only got when Merry was in trouble. He had learned long ago not to ignore his gut reactions, especially where his wife was concerned. She had a habit of involving herself in dangerous situations, investigating where she had no business. Although he admitted to himself that her amateur sleuthing had solved a mystery or two in the past, it was never without peril.

He glanced at his watch then read the sign on the door. Of course, Sunday. The shop was closed. He'd been so busy he couldn't keep track of what day of the week it was. So where was she? There wasn't any answer when he phoned home; not even the boys were there. Hmm, that means they were probably at the Thompson's house.

Hopping back into his cruiser, he drove over to Anna and Chuck's house. A quick rap on the door and Anna let him in.

Billy and Johnny tromped up the steps from the family room with their friend Stevie.

"Hey Dad," Billy greeted his father.

"You guys know where your mother is?" Doug hated to ask.

"Dunno exactly. She told us she was doing something with that reporter. Can we stay longer? We were in the middle of the battle for planet Mars," Johnny said as the boys looked ready to leap down the stairs and return to their video game.

"Yeah, I guess so. Okay with you, Anna?"

"No problem," Anna replied and tried not to meet Doug's eyes. He'd know in an instant that she knew exactly what Meredith and Trixie had gotten themselves into.

"It's a trapdoor," I breathed.

We pulled on the hinged door, lifting it and then dropping it to the side. A black gaping hole opened below us.

"After you," she said with a shaky grin.

"Do you think it's safe? Dare we?" I pointed my flashlight into the dark pit, seeing steps leading into the damp darkness.

"Sure."

Carefully, we descended into the lower level, our footsteps echoing off cold stone walls. The steps ended in a vault-like chamber lit only by the glow of our flashlights. I coughed in the close, musty air. My breath appeared like white fog in the freezing subterranean temperatures. We hesitated, stood rooted to the spot, then Trixie grabbed my hand.

"I hear something. Listen. Do you think there are rats down here?" Trixie questioned.

"Probably. If something runs across my foot, I'll be out of here in two seconds."

Pointing my flashlight into the small space, I shone it along the walls and floor, foot by foot, stopping as it illuminated an object.

Along the far wall stood a squat stand, its wood rotten and cracked, holding a bundle covered with oilcloth. Cautiously, I took the few steps toward the table. Peeling back the cloth, my light shone on what appeared to be a thick leather-bound book.

I reached out; the cracked leather felt cool beneath my fingertips.

"What is it?" Trixie asked.

I opened the cover. The pages inside appeared yellowed but intact. Shining my light onto the book, I read aloud the handwritten names scrolled in faint ink on the first page — Reverend Amos Kirkland, Eli Maxwell, Luther Bradley Johnson. I gasped at the name Bradley included among the founders.

"The pages are stuck together from the dampness. If I try pulling them apart, I'll damage the paper. We'll have to get it out of here before examining it," I told Trixie, my teeth chattering in the cold.

A sudden creak above made us both freeze.

Footsteps.

Trixie killed the light. We stood in the pitch-dark tomb.

"Merry?" Doug's voice echoed faintly from the trapdoor.

We both exhaled.

"Down here," I called up, turning on my flashlight. "You will not believe what we just found." I couldn't keep the excitement out of my voice.

Doug's boots thudded against the stone stairs as he made his way down, his eyes narrowing at the sight of the open journal.

"Of all the crazy stunts ... what if something happened to the two of you? You could have been trapped down here."

"We were perfectly safe," I said in our defense, my toe kicking a loose stone.

"Uh-huh, somehow I doubt that."

"How did you know where to find us?" I asked.

"Saw your car parked next to the church. I told you not to interfere in my investigation."

I could hear the anger simmering below the surface and the strained control in Doug's voice.

He gave Trixie a warning glare before turning back to me. "Anything else down here? If not, get that book and bring it up to the surface. Let's get out of here, now."

"This is going to make a fabulous story for the paper," Trixie said, her voice bubbling over in enthusiasm.

"Do you think you should announce the existence of the journal? What if someone tries to steal it? You've already been broken into once." I said as we climbed the stairs up to the base of the tower.

"This is too good of a story to keep quiet. We've got to thoroughly inspect that journal. Maybe it's what Bradley was searching for and why he killed Alvin Maxwell. Did you notice the Maxwell name among the founders? Suppose there's a claim to land based upon that original deed? This could change the entire town!" Trixie speculated.

"You don't even know if there is a deed mentioned in that book. What if it only points us to another clue, another *silent bell*. I still say hiding an important journal in a church bell tower is too obvious. Why wasn't it found before this?"

Trixie and I climbed into my SUV, the book on her lap, as we followed Doug back to the sheriff's office at his insistence. It wasn't my idea. I wanted to take the book to the town hall and the mayor's office. Once we got to Doug's office, I planned on phoning my aunt. Looking over at Trixie, I saw she was already narrating notes into her phone for her next big newsflash.

I couldn't help wondering ... where would this lead us? Was Carl Bradley really searching for the missing journal, or is there more? And where is the history professor now?

A lone figure hid in the shadows behind the old tower wall, watching the two women drive away with the exact ledger he sought. But there were other ways; it would be his soon. He had to bide his time.

Chapter Eleven

Iron Pledge

"What's this all about?" asked Fran as she rushed into the sheriff's station. She ignored the front desk officer and went straight back to Doug's office.

"Madam Mayor, I see someone has notified you of the historic find," Doug said as he waved her into the room.

I snorted at my husband's formality as he addressed my aunt.

Fran glanced between me, Trixie, and Doug before she focused on the object lying in the center of his desk. The leather-bound book, covered in thick dust, smelled like a dank root cellar.

"We found a journal written by Meadowood's founding fathers. The pages are too stuck together to probe beyond the front cover," I said.

Fran stepped forward and fingered the ancient tome. She lifted the cover; her eyes widened as she read the names scrolled on the top parchment page.

"This book needs to be handled with care. And by someone who trained in dealing with rare artifacts. I know just the right person," Fran said with a smile and a look of determination on her face.

I watched my aunt as she lifted her cell phone from her jacket pocket and began tapping in a number.

"Hello. Ms. Moore, this is Mayor Andrews in Meadowood. We need your services. Are you free to examine a recently discovered relic?" She listened to the reply on the other end of the line. "Yes. Perfect. I look forward to seeing you tomorrow in my office."

Fran ended the call, then faced Doug. "I have an expert who deals with art and rare antiquities. She will examine the book tomorrow. Please don't handle it anymore until she arrives."

"Is that the same Susan Moore that you interviewed for the director's position?" I asked.

"Yes it is. We should have given her the job to begin with and if she's still willing, I plan to do so. Susan is accustomed to dealing with fine art. She'll know the best way to examine this fragile book and paper."

"Great. Can we watch? I mean Trixie and me. We've got a vested interest in the book; after all, we were the ones who found it."

Under lock and key in a special climate-controlled room of the museum, the ancient leather-bound book and its fragile parchment pages lay atop a velvet-draped worktable. Sunlight streamed through the narrow windows in slanted rays that caught the faintest flecks of dust in the air. They kept the room cool and dry—perfect conditions for delicate historical work.

Susan Moore stood in the center of it all, hands wearing white cotton gloves, her dark hair tied back into a no-nonsense bun. Her hazel eyes sparkled behind tortoiseshell glasses as she examined the fragile book with reverent care. Previously the head curator for the Sevierville Museum of Art, Susan had been among the finalists for the museum director in Meadowood. That was before Carl Bradley had swooped in with doctorate credentials and a phony background. Now, ironically, the town needed her more than ever.

"This binding is early 19th century," she said softly, mostly to herself. "Likely calfskin, hand-tooled. Remarkably preserved considering where it was hidden."

Fran, Trixie, and I stood nearby, silently observing. Trixie had even tucked away her ever-present notebook for the moment.

Fran crossed her arms. "Susan, we don't want to damage anything, but we need answers. The people of Meadowood deserve to know what's in that book."

Susan nodded. "And they will. But you don't rush history."

With the delicacy of a surgeon, she used a bone folder to loosen the front cover, which creaked faintly but did not resist. The smell of old leather, ink, and earth rose from the spine—a scent that spoke of centuries and secrets.

She used a portable humidification chamber to lightly moisten the glued edges of the pages that had fused over time, applying a fine mist through a mesh screen.

Trixie wrinkled her nose. "Smells like wet parchment and moss."

"Because that's what it is," Susan said with a small smile. "The vellum reacts best when eased slowly. Rushing this process could destroy half the writing."

She peeled apart the first two pages with tweezers. The ink, faded but legible, covered the page in looping calligraphy.

I leaned forward. "What's it say?"

Susan adjusted her magnifier. "It's dated July 9th, 1818. There's a list of names— Reverend Amos Kirkland, Eli Maxwell, Luther Bradley Johnson, and a few others. There's a heading: *Pledge of Iron, Sworn Beneath Heaven's Eye.*"

Fran looked on in wonder. "Those are the town's founding families."

I gasped softly. "This ... this is their pact, like the message in the desk talked about ... the Iron Pledge."

"You better show Susan and me the paper you found in that desk. Let Susan read the message," Fran directed.

I handed the slip of parchment paper to the curator. She studied it and then turned her focus back onto the leather journal.

Susan nodded as she read the faded ink. "They swore to protect the boundaries of what they called the Kirkland Tract—hundreds of acres that likely encompass modern-day Meadowood and stretch into the mineral-rich northern ridges. They agreed that the land, water access, and its resources were not to be sold or divided outside their families without unanimous consent. The pact kept the land from being sold to outsiders or exploited for profit."

"Mineral rights," Trixie breathed. "So that's what this is all about."

Susan turned another page. "It's more than that. The next page shows a map with instructions for finding the original deeds of each founder. There's mention of a cave system and natural springs believed to have healing properties. And this—" she pointed to a stylized symbol etched in red ink, the same one we had found on the beam in the bell tower. "—is the seal of the Iron Pledge."

Trixie looked like she was vibrating with journalistic energy. "How cool is this! We're going on a bonafide treasure hunt to find those deeds. This could change everything. Land use, water control, local politics—"

"Whoa! Slow down girl. Come down to earth," I said.

"You're right, it could change everything. Which is exactly why we can't go printing it just yet," Fran interrupted, her voice firm. "Until we verify every name and detail, this stays between us. Trixie, I'm asking you to hold off on printing your story."

Trixie frowned but nodded reluctantly. "I don't like sitting on a scoop, but I understand."

"If you tell people there's a map and secret deeds, folks will start digging up the streets of this town. It will cause chaos," the mayor cautioned.

"If there's any treasure hunting to be conducted, it will be under the auspices of the sheriff's office and controlled. We can't have people putting themselves in danger crawling through tunnels or digging up basements. And I mean everyone, even you, Merry," Doug spoke up for the first time as he observed the procedure.

Susan continued painstakingly cataloging the pages while I assisted her by photographing and logging every segment. As the hours passed, it became clear that the Iron Pledge had been more than symbolic—it had shaped Meadowood's entire foundation.

As the last page came loose, Susan removed her gloves and stood straight. Her hands were trembling ... not from fatigue, but from awe.

"It's all here," she said. "A map detailing where to unearth the original deeds. The founders' signatures. Even encoded language on how to break the pact, if necessary. That may take me weeks to decipher. But this ..." she touched the open book lightly, as if it were sacred, "... is the most important historical discovery Meadowood has seen in over a century."

Fran turned to face her, eyes shining with calm conviction. "Susan Moore, I know this is sudden, but I want you to take over as director of the museum. Effective immediately. We can't have it shut down while Carl Bradley is missing. And frankly, this place needs someone who respects its history and art as much as you do."

Susan's eyes widened. "Mayor Andrews ... I, um, are you sure?"

"Absolutely. The executive committee will back me. Carl's disappearance, combined with the mounting evidence in Alvin Maxwell's death, is reason enough for his removal. We need transparency, integrity, and dedication. You've got all three."

Susan looked around the room: the table, the artifacts, the eager faces. She took a breath and smiled.

"Then I accept. I'm honored. Let's show the citizens of Meadowood what history can teach us."

I exchanged a glance with Trixie, and for the first time in days, felt a flicker of hope.

Secrets were coming to light. Justice might still be served. And through it all, the museum and my aunt's vision stood as a beacon ... not only of what the town had been, but of what it could become.

Outside, the brisk autumn wind whistled in the chapel tower, sending a faint echo through the museum's open courtyard.

The silent bell had spoken.

Chapter Twelve

Trick or Treat

Georgia Simmons stormed into the mayor's office. If she had been a dragon, you would have seen the smoke billowing out of her nose and the flames shooting from her eyes. The mayor's secretary, Dottie, rushed in behind her. She wrung her hands and tried to apologize to her boss.

"I'm sorry Mayor Andrews; she insisted."

"That's okay Dottie. Have a seat, Georgia. What can I do for you?" Fran said. Her secretary gratefully returned to her own desk.

"What is Susan Moore doing in our history museum? I demand to know what's happening," Georgia's strident voice rose with each word.

"I hired her for the director's position last night. She's going to prepare the museum for opening to the public. Ms. Moore has provided a valuable service and assisted this community."

"But what about Carl Bradley?" Georgia kept insisting.

"You must have heard the gossip around town. The man has fled. He's wanted for murdering Alvin Maxwell," Fran said.

"But ... but ... he has a PhD! He can't be a murderer. My nephew would never hurt ... I mean Dr. Bradley." Georgia reasoned as if that should proclaim his innocence.

"I'm sure the real Carl Bradley may hold that doctorate, but we only have this man's word that he is whom he claims to be. Meadowood needs someone with integrity. Susan Moore is my choice and I've made my decision. I've already received the majority of the town council votes approving her."

"Well! If that's the way you want it. You're the mayor!" she huffed and sprung from her chair. No easy feat for someone so overweight.

"Yes. That's right. I am the mayor and my choice stands." Fran shook her head as the woman marched out of the office and slammed the door behind her.

"Heard you had a run in with the delightful Georgia Simmons this morning," Anna drawled, then laughed.

"Let's just say she made her opinion known," Fran said, reaching for her teacup. She sighed. It had been a long day, and the day wasn't over yet.

"Do you think Carl Bradley knew about the pact?" Trixie asked as she sipped a cup of Earl Grey tea.

It was late afternoon, and the tea shop was closed. We had gathered to discuss the impact of the leather journal and Susan Moore replacing Bradley at the museum.

"Well, he was a history professor in that college; he could have researched Meadowood's history and learned the names of the founding families. Aunt Fran, you said Carl was interested in the S.O.F.M. He could have learned about the pact there," I said.

Pouring hot Earl Grey tea from my favorite ceramic pot decorated in a delicate rose pattern, I freshened everyone's cups. Anna sat listening and absorbing our recitation of the journal's information. Colleen wore a worried expression on her face.

"Would Carl Bradley murder Alvin Maxwell just because that journal mentioned his ancestors? I hate to think the poor man died because a moldy book listed his name," Colleen said.

Her words made us all pause.

"I'm ashamed to admit I had forgotten Alvin in the excitement of hunting for the documents described in the journal. You're right, Colleen. Alvin was likely killed because his family could lay claim to a tract of Meadowood land or whatever wealth it created. What was it that Alvin told you, Trixie, the day before the party?" I asked.

Trixie dug into her handbag and pulled out the small notebook she always carried. Flipping through the pages, her fingers stopped at the interview she had with Alvin on October 27th.

"Alvin told me he found a box with old documents from the 1820s. Copies of deeds with land ownership disputes involving the founding families — Maxwell, Johnson, even the old Kirkland estate. Alvin believed Bradley hid the evidence of those claims. He said Bradley was looking for a vault or records room that he hadn't accessed yet. Of course we know now that Bradley didn't find that vault ... we did under the bell tower. I don't think the director was hiding evidence of the original claims, he was searching for them."

"Why? What would he have to gain?" asked Anna as she reached for a raisin bran muffin.

"Good question. I keep thinking of the names recorded in that journal: Amos Kirkland, Eli Maxwell, and Luther Bradley Johnson. Do you think Carl Bradley traced his heritage back to Luther Johnson? Is Bradley a family surname? Perhaps a maternal surname used back then? Maybe he wants the Meadowood deeds for his family?" I suggested.

"Definite possibility," Trixie said, munching on a cookie. "I'd like to know what name Bradley used before his tenure at Fairview. Why did he change his name? What is he hiding?"

"I think the man's a phony. Why else would someone use a false identity?" I asked. I planned on digging until I hit pay dirt.

"Has anyone spoken to Teresa?" Anna asked, changing the subject.

"I called her after Susan Moore finished work on the journal. I wanted her to know about the Maxwell name mentioned there and the potential land claims," Fran stated.

"How is she?" I asked before swallowing a piece of bran muffin.

"The medical examiner is releasing Alvin's body to the family. She told me that a funeral service would be held tomorrow at Wagner's," Fran said. A moment of silence fell over our group.

Finally, I spoke, mirroring the thoughts we all had in mind. "You know, this may be the first time I've ever felt like I just wanted to get Halloween over with and put it behind me. Makes me feel guilty, denying the kids their fun. But honestly, I can't even think of trick or treat with everything else that's been going on."

"I'd have to agree with you, however, it is Halloween and nothing we do will stop that. We better get a move on and dash home to prepare for the little goblins," Anna said.

I rose and carried the teapot into the kitchen. Anna followed me with our dishes and a plate of muffins. We quickly bagged the leftover muffins and took care of the dirty dishes.

Colleen and Trixie put the chairs back around the table, and Aunt Fran gathered up the paper napkins we had used.

"Thanks for your help. Guess I'll see you all later or tomorrow at the funeral," I said.

"This is going to be a long Halloween night. I can't help but feel something ominous is in the air, lurking among the children trick or treating tonight," Fran said as she pulled on her coat.

A full moon cast its pearly light over the darkened avenues. Meadowood glimmered with amber bulbs in coach lanterns on poles lining the center streets. The orange glow of carved pumpkins flickered from nearly every porch along Park, Elm, and Oak Streets. Their jagged smiles and triangle eyes cast dancing shadows across sidewalks strewn with crunchy oak and maple leaves. A brisk wind blew, tossing the leaves into the air only to scatter again when they settled to earth by children running down the sidewalk. Witches and ghosts paraded down the street, accompanied by spacemen, cowboys, football players, and fairy princesses. Giggles, squeals of laughter, cheerful voices, rode the stiff breeze as children rang doorbells and made their way from house to house. The smell of cinnamon apples, warm doughnuts, and faint wood smoke from chimneys mingled with the chilly October air.

"Mroww," Mittens meowed contentedly, stretched out along the back of a recliner. The feline lazily washed his orange and white tabby face and flicked his tail as he watched the commotion out the window.

I positioned myself near our front door with a large bowl of candy bars to hand out to the scampering goblins.

Billy and Johnny had dashed out in costume earlier to meet friends and gather their treats. Billy was in high spirits as usual, but I couldn't help but notice that Johnny acted more subdued, almost bored. My young teen was growing out of the childish event. This would likely be his last year for trick or treating on Halloween. That thought made me sad.

Pots of golden mums adorned our front steps next to a pair of jack-o'-lanterns that the boys had carved. Candles shone through the sinister eyes and jagged teeth. It was the only decorating that I had bothered to do this year. In the past, cornstalks and a scarecrow stood proudly in our yard. This year, I really wasn't in the mood to go all out; what with all the museum and mysterious historical records consuming my mind, not to mention a dead body.

Beneath the candy-coated cheer of Halloween night, Meadowood was still a town in mourning. Only three days had passed since Alvin Maxwell's death at the masquerade party. Although the evidence pointed to Bradley as his suspected killer, he was still at large. Apprehension filled the air. People moved cautiously and looked at everyone suspiciously.

Town wounds were fresh, the loss etched into every hesitant smile. Despite the grief, the townsfolk had made an effort to celebrate for the children's sake: draping spider webs on shop windows, setting up hay bale photo booths, and organizing a costume contest outside the town hall. But an invisible weight seemed to press down on every citizen.

At the closed Meadowood History Museum, the flickering coach lanterns flanking the front door burned softly against the teal clapboard and brick exterior. Inside, however, the museum was dark.

Too dark.

A shadow moved past the front window.

A tiny *click* echoed in the night as a side window, pried open with methodical force, swung upward. A figure dressed in black slid inside, landing lightly on the hardwood floor.

The intruder moved with purpose, gloved hands brushing past framed exhibits and glass display cases. A flashlight flicked on briefly, just enough to check labels.

His breath fogged in the chill interior. Each step echoed faintly.

His movements grew faster, more desperate, as he bypassed rooms filled with artifacts and display signage.

A low curse escaped the figure's lips.

The journal and map to the deeds were gone.

The robber opened cabinet drawers. Empty. He searched beneath the desk in newly appointed Susan Moore's office. Nothing.

In the silence, a distant Halloween whistle carried through the open window ... some child in the street with a noisemaker. The thief flinched.

After several more frantic minutes, he backed away from the curator's desk and slipped out the way he had come.

The museum remained undisturbed to the casual eye, but inside, one case had a cracked hinge. Another drawer lay open and askew. The alarm system, still waiting to be updated by the city, had not been triggered.

The following morning, Susan Moore opened the museum under her tutelage for the first time. Walking among the exhibits, turning on lights, gliding her fingers across glass cases ... she discovered signs of the break-in. She immediately phoned the sheriff's office. Sheriff Douglas Gardner arrived with a team, inspecting the scene.

A deputy dusted for fingerprints along the edges of window frames and on the discovered open drawer front. Black powder coated the glass case cracked by the robber. Forensics searched for prints but found none. The culprit had worn gloves. The team recovered a tiny fiber, little more than a thread, from the frame of one window.

The new museum director watched the proceedings. She wrung her hands as she faced the sheriff.

"Nothing taken," Susan confirmed. "Luckily, the journal was still locked in your office gun safe."

Doug nodded, jaw tight. "Whoever this was, he was looking for something very specific. Probably that journal, and he or she thought it would be here. I'd like to know how the thief knew about the book. It was supposed to be a secret. The mayor didn't want it announced to the town yet."

Susan hesitated. "Do you think it was Carl Bradley? Would he come back for the journal?"

Doug shook his head slowly. "I don't know. If he was crazy enough to kill for it, he'd be daring enough to commit burglary."

He didn't say what they were both thinking: If it wasn't Carl ... then who else wanted those documents badly enough to break into a museum on Halloween night?

Susan looked shaken but gathered her reserve. "I'll speak with the mayor. We need that alarm system active now. I don't feel the journal would be safe if I keep it in the museum."

"I agree," Doug said. "We'll store it in the sheriff department for now. I'll have a deputy posted at the museum overnight too."

"Thank you," Susan said with a nod of her head as she glanced around at the black fingerprint powder that would need removing.

Merry tapped on the door. A deputy allowed her in; it was easier than trying to argue with the sheriff's wife. She usually got her way in the end.

Doug looked up as his wife entered the museum. "I wondered how long it would take you to show up here. The grapevine must be slipping if it took you almost two hours after the call came in."

Merry held in a chuckle, rolling her eyes at her husband. "Well you need to consider that Teresa has the salon closed."

"Ahh ... that would explain it," Doug said with a grin.

"Can I see what happened?"

"Sure, check the place out. I'd like your opinion. You spent time in here during the open house. See anything out of place?"

Merry nodded and then walked the halls of the museum, slowly taking in the slight damage, and noted the places covered in black powder from forensics.

"It doesn't feel like a robbery," she said to Doug as they stood near the crooked drawer. "It feels ... personal."

Doug gave her a look. "You thinking what I'm thinking?"

"That someone doesn't want the truth getting out," Merry replied. "Maybe someone connected to one of the founding families. Or even an outsider who's learned more than they should."

She paused at the cracked hinge of a display case housing Kirkland's original compass.

"They weren't looking for jewelry or cash," she said. "They wanted answers. Or they wanted to bury them."

Doug exhaled slowly. "Then we better dig deeper. Before they try again."

Chapter Thirteen

Condolences

Anna and I locked the tea room door. We decided to walk the two blocks over to Wagner's Funeral Home on Elm Avenue; likely we wouldn't have found a parking spot, anyway. Temperatures had dropped overnight, although today's blue sky and sunshine were deceiving. I stuffed my hands in my coat pockets as we walked.

John Wagner and his family had served the Meadowood community for over fifty years. Wagner's Funeral Home occupied a Victorian mansion, three-stories high and complete with round turrets on the corners of the roof. The only thing missing to complete the gothic image was a pair of gargoyles. The somber building wore pewter gray siding with black-trimmed windows. Wagner's house had once been home to a wealthy investor in the late 1800s. Like many massive older homes, they were impossible to heat or cool and wound up being sold to businesses for commercial use.

Cars lined each side of Elm and along both intersecting side streets. As we neared the building, I saw that the parking lot was filled to capacity too.

"Good thing we left the car back at the tea shop," Anna said.

"I knew there would be a big turnout. The Maxwell name is well-known throughout the entire county," I said as we approached the tall flight of granite steps leading to the front entrance.

A rush of warm air enveloped us as we entered the wide doors of the funeral parlor. The welcome heat soon became stuffy and cloying in the close confines. Throngs of people stood speaking softly or shuffling around to greet others they hadn't seen in ages or not since the last community event. We inched our way forward in a slow-moving line toward the guest book resting upon a dark walnut lectern. Rows of signatures filled the pages. My eyes scanned the names, recognizing most before I signed my name and expressed condolences from the entire Gardner family. Handing the pen to Anna, I stood aside so she could do the same.

Waves of heavy cologne from over a hundred people mixed with sweet floral fragrances radiating from the adjoining room. Multiple baskets displayed striking arrangements of purple asters, orange dahlias, red zinnias, and chrysanthemums of every color tucked into sprays of autumn leaves. The combined scent clung to the heated atmosphere.

People packed the visitation room and lobby. I could hardly move within the crowd. Most of Meadowood must be present plus folks from Pottstown, where Alvin had worked in one of the factories. His friends and coworkers had come out in force to show their respect.

Heavy navy-blue brocaded draperies were drawn closed across a triple-wide window. Several rows of folding chairs had been set up on the plush slate-colored carpeting in the middle of the spacious room, with comfortable sofas and brocade side chairs arranged along the outer walls. Every chair was occupied, leaving standing room only, and that was a tight fit. I nudged Anna and pointed toward the left side of the room where Colleen and Ron stood chatting with Barb and Ted Williams.

"I'm going to speak with Teresa," I said. I elbowed my way with words of "excuse me" and "pardon me" as I wove through the mass.

Teresa sat with her head bowed as I approached. Her flaming orange hair stood out against her black mourning dress, painting her like a Halloween caricature, however unintended.

"Teresa, I'm so sorry. Alvin was a wonderful man and the entire community will miss him," I said softly as I reached out and patted her arm.

She raised tearful eyes, swollen from crying, and nodded. "You find out who did this to my brother! You hear me, Merry? We both know it had to do with that museum and the Maxwell family history. I deserve the truth and to see justice done." She squeezed my hand in a firm grip, not releasing me until I nodded in agreement.

"I'll do whatever I can. Trust me," I said. Giving her a quick hug, I moved away from her and the bronze coffin where Alvin lay in eternal sleep, his hands folded across his chest.

Clark Penner brushed against me in the crowded room. A diminutive man, always needing to prove his importance, I'd had the misfortune to do business with him in the past.

Turning to him, I offered a polite greeting. "Hello Clark."

"Heard you're sticking your nose into police business again. About time the people that deserve recognition in this town get it. Don't get in the way, or you'll regret it," Penner said then blended into the crowd.

What was that about? I wondered, staring after the man's back.

Inching my way back toward the lobby, I heard my name called above the murmur of voices filling the room. Aunt Fran waved as she navigated the crowd toward me. The mayor smiled and greeted people as she went.

"Whew! This place is unbelievable," Fran said as she managed to gain my side.

"I know. So many people, I don't know half of them. Must be

Alvin's friends from Pottstown or family members from out of town."

"Looks like everyone from Meadowood is here," Fran said. She gazed about the packed room, then stopped. I saw her eyebrows shoot up and a frown crease her forehead as she stared at a gathering of men.

"What is it? Who did you see?" I asked my aunt.

"So many people ... I'm not sure, but I thought I recognized Byron Adams. No ... probably not. Maybe just someone who looks like him."

"Are you sure? Which one? Point him out to me."

My aunt turned and scanned the throng again, then shook her head. "I don't see him now. It isn't likely that Byron Adams would attend a funeral service for a perfect stranger. I must be mistaken."

"Trust your instincts. If you think you saw this Mister Adams, then you did. What was the reason he gave you for quitting the director's position?" I asked as we continued to inch toward the entrance.

"He told me he'd been offered a better job in Boston, at one of the prestigious museums. Received a call based on a previous application. Naturally, Meadowood can't compete with the higher salary range proposed by a big city. If it was Adams I saw, why isn't he in Boston and what would he be doing here?" Fran said in a low voice for my ears alone.

Later that night, I stared at my computer screen, my mind blank. The house was silent ... the boys in bed and only Mittens purring thrummed next to me. Outside, the wind blew, stripping tree branches bare and scattering leaves. My sweet mug of lavender and chamomile tea sat next to me, steam rising, forgotten. I propped my chin in my palm and tried to make sense of the information before me.

Doug entered the kitchen, closing the back door and locking up for the night, then dragged his tired feet into the laundry room where he hung his holster and belt. After placing his revolver in the gun safe, he completed his regular routine. He wandered into the kitchen, felt the coffee pot to see if it was still hot, then poured himself a mug.

"You're lost in thought. What are you working on?" he asked as he settled onto a stool at the counter and leaned over to study my screen.

"Hmm? Oh, it's just this thing with Carl Bradley. Trixie and I both searched for background information on the man but couldn't find any reference to him outside Fairview College. I didn't even find him among the alumni names listed in the University of Pennsylvania. It's like he's a ghost. Weird!"

"Email me what information you have. I'll look into it. Right now, I just want a hot shower and a soft bed," Doug said with a yawn.

The fluorescent lights hummed in the Meadowood Sheriff's Department evidence room as Sheriff Doug Gardner leaned over the stainless steel worktable, examining the bloodstained cane. Forensics had confirmed the blood on the cane plus blood found on a jagged brick both belonged to Alvin Maxwell. It was likely that the perpetrator hit Alvin with the cane, perhaps knocking him down, but likely administered the final killing blow with the heavier brick.

The cane's curved silver handle caught the light like a mirror, but Doug's eyes focused on the dark patches of dried blood and the smooth shaft where, just maybe, a set of prints had been preserved.

Deputy Tony Dalton stood beside him, adjusting his gloves. "We've got solid ridges on three sections," he said, carefully powdering the cane with black magnetic dust.

Doug gave a curt nod. "Let's get clean tape lifts and run them against what we pulled from the museum office. We need to confirm that Carl Bradley had his hands on this cane the night of the masquerade and at the crime scene. We know he dressed in the Phantom of the Opera costume ... if it's his prints on this cane, and the cane is confirmed as the murder weapon, then it means he killed Alvin. Yeah, I know ... thin."

Tony arched an eyebrow as he secured the clear tape onto the powder-dusted prints. "Assuming Bradley took off the gloves he wore at the party."

"Yeah," Doug said, his voice low. "Assuming."

The digital scanner in the corner beeped slightly as Tony fed the lifted prints into the machine. On the monitor, a magnified swirl of whorls and ridges appeared, followed by the comparative fingerprint scans retrieved from the museum break-in—specifically from the corner of the director's desk drawer.

"Got a match," Tony confirmed after a few tense moments. "Right index and middle finger. Same print on the cane as the one on the museum drawer."

Doug crossed his arms. "Bradley's prints on his museum desk is where we'd expect to find them since the man was acting director. It doesn't tie him to the break-in, but it helps to confirm the prints' identity. And he carried this cane at the masquerade party."

Tony gave him a sidelong glance. "But the man is still missing, either skipped town or met foul play. You still want to run the prints through the federal database?"

Doug nodded. "Yeah. Something's off about this guy. No digital footprint older than ten years. That's not normal for someone who claims to hold a Ph.D. in history and a university record."

Tony logged into the National Criminal Information Center system and uploaded the fingerprint data.

They waited in silence as the progress bar loaded, slowly and methodically.

Finally, a window popped open.

MATCH FOUND.

Doug leaned in, reading aloud.

"Name: Harold Foreman. Multiple arrests for fraud, identity theft, embezzlement. Last known address: Fort Wayne, Indiana. Last conviction: ten years ago."

Tony let out a low whistle. "So Carl Bradley doesn't exist. Or at least, he isn't the guy the town hired."

Doug's jaw tightened. "He was hiding in plain sight. Used a stolen name and credentials to embed himself in a town museum. And killed to protect his secret and plans to steal from the town."

He stared at the monitor, the mugshot of Harold Foreman glaring back with a smug smirk, years younger but unmistakably the man they knew as Carl Bradley.

Tony shook his head. "This explains why no one from Fairview College could verify his employment. They probably had no clue who he really was."

Doug turned toward the file cabinet and pulled out the evidence binder, flipping it open to the museum theft and Maxwell murder reports. "We need to issue a bulletin. Use both names: Harold Foreman aka Carl Bradley. Get his face on every law enforcement database east of the Mississippi."

Tony was already typing. "Want to send an alert to the Ohio Historical Society too? If he's been stealing artifacts under assumed names, they might have a list of other aliases."

"Good thinking. Do it."

Doug stared at the screen again. The pieces were finally fitting, but the picture they formed was darker than he'd anticipated.

"Get me everything we can find on Harold Foreman. Biography, criminal timeline, known associates. I want to know where he's been, what he's stolen, and who helped him."

Tony nodded, still typing. "I'll reach out to Fort Wayne PD and pull his arrest records. If he had a lawyer or an accomplice, we'll know soon."

Doug rubbed his temples. "He had to have a reason for coming to Meadowood. The journal's *Iron Pledge*. The land deeds. He wasn't just interested in history ... he was looking for power. Or big money."

Tony looked up from the screen. "What if he wasn't working alone?"

Doug didn't answer right away. He walked to the evidence board and pinned the photo of the cane beside the photo of the leather journal, then drew a red line connecting them.

"Then we've got bigger problems," he mumbled. "Because whoever helped him ... might still be out there."

Outside, the wind picked up, rattling the old windowpanes of the sheriff's office. A storm was moving in, and with it ... trouble.

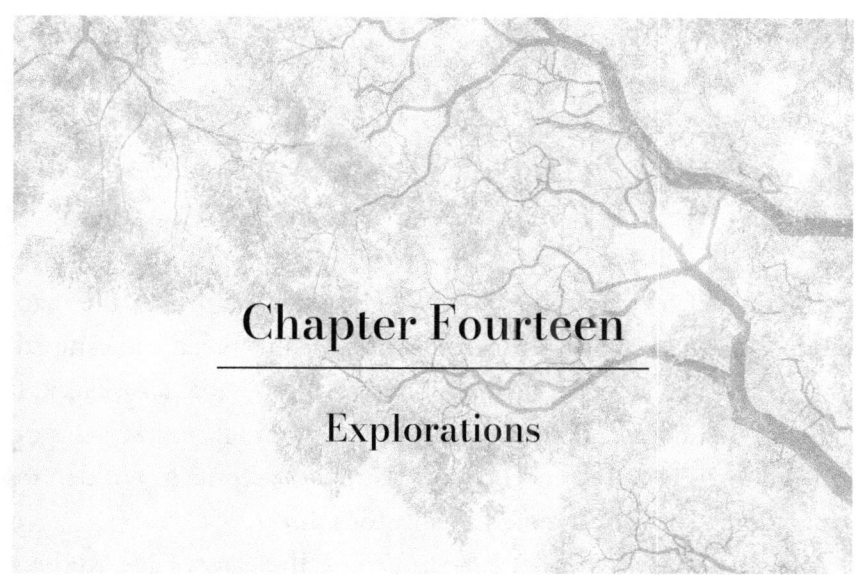

Chapter Fourteen

Explorations

I t had been three days since Doug's team confirmed Carl Bradley was Harold Foreman, and the revelation hadn't sat quietly. It buzzed in the back of my mind like an angry hornet. He hadn't just killed Alvin Maxwell ... he'd tried to rewrite Meadowood's entire history for his own gain.

Trixie and I sat at my kitchen table the next morning. Photos that I had snapped of the map, when assisting Susan Moore's restoration of the historic journal, now lay printed in large quadrants and taped together like a giant puzzle.

"Does Doug know you kept these?" asked Trixie.

"No, that is ... no one said I had to delete them off my phone. I took a picture of each journal page as back up during the process and to record Moore's procedure. I just figured the close ups of the map would come in handy."

The tea kettle whistled in the background, and the scent of cinnamon from leftover tea shop scones lingered in the air. But there was no comfort in my steaming mug today.

"I've stared at these shots so long I'm seeing double," I muttered, tracing my finger along the jagged edge of the Fox Run River pictured on the map. I put my magnifying glass next to the map.

"Here," Trixie said, tapping the spot near the map's lower corner. "See the symbol? It's the same iron emblem we found carved onto the beam in the bell tower. Looks like an upside-down triangle with a dot in the middle."

"The seal of the *Iron Pledge*," I whispered, staring at the map photo. "It's marked near the caves. My cub scouts hiked and camped in that park and all over that land for years. I know that area. Heck, I grew up around here. When I was a kid, two boys from my class got lost in those caves. Ted and I always warned the scouts in our den to avoid them. Those caves posed a dangerous threat."

Trixie leaned closer, her breath fogging the glass of her reading glasses. "If we're reading this right, the symbol sits just east of Fox Run Park. That's where the council wanted to mine a couple years ago."

I nodded. "Yeah, the men in the S.O.F.M. pushed hard for that agreement ... said the mineral deposits were valuable and would bring revenue to the town. But the citizens rallied against it. Environmental risk. Fran proved it. She even campaigned against mining that land. It went to a town vote. They banned fracking. You remember, it was during our bicentennial celebration."

"And now we know why Carl, I mean Harold, was so obsessed with the *Iron Pledge*." Trixie tapped the ledger photos. "The journal proclaimed the founding families and future families held the land in trust. Any sale or mineral lease required unanimous approval by all descendants."

"But the Kirklands are gone, no living relatives," I added. "Alvin was the sole Maxwell male descendant. If Foreman wanted control of the land, removing Alvin would eliminate a key vote."

"And if he posed as a Johnson descendant," Trixie said slowly, "he'd have the majority."

I sat back, feeling the weight of it. "Maybe that's what he had planned. He was trying to steal Meadowood's land for the money."

Trixie's eyes gleamed with a reporter's spark. "And now we're going to find the evidence he didn't want anyone else to see."

The forecast said possible snow, and the wind already carried the smell of winter ... sharp, moist, and full of warning. We layered up: heavy coats, wool scarves, gloves stuffed in pockets. I grabbed two flashlights, a scout compass, water, and food, and shoved it all into a backpack. I pulled on the thick-soled hiking boots Doug had given me last Christmas.

"If we're doing this, we better leave while we have any decent daylight. There's not much sun shining through this overcast sky," I said.

"Okay. Let's do it. This is going to be my lead story in the next issue of the Meadowood Flyer," Trixie said with a huge smile across her face.

Before leaving the house, I left Doug a note on the counter to let him know my plans. Just in case of trouble, then locked the door.

Mittens eyed the scrap of paper on the counter, batting it with his paw like a new toy. The paper floated down and slid across the tiled floor; the cat pounced and chased the paper, his claws shredding part of the note.

We climbed into my SUV and headed out of town toward the scout campground, the old Granger's farm, and the park.

"Ready?" I asked as we stood at the edge of the woods behind Fox Run Park. I parked my car in the gravel lot farthest away from the scout jamboree camp and near the entrance of the forest. Grabbing the small backpack, I shifted the straps on my shoulders to balance the weight.

Trixie cracked her knuckles. "Born ready. But if we get eaten by bears, I want a full-page tribute in the Gazette."

I laughed. "There aren't any bears in this area and if there were, they'd be starting their winter hibernation by now."

"Got everything?" Trixie smirked, eyeing my full backpack.

"Hey, what can I say? I'm still a den mother at heart and scouts are always prepared. You'll thank me later if you need a bottle of water or get hungry for that protein bar."

The trees creaked under the weight of new frost, their bare branches brittle and silvered. We hiked through stands of oak and pine trees deeper into the woods. The map's coordinates had led us to a narrow trail, half-forgotten, no longer maintained, that curved up toward a ridge lined with outcrops of dark stone. I stopped and peered up at the sun, checked the compass, and tried to get our bearings.

We moved cautiously, boots crunching leaves and hardened mud; scant sunlight pierced the growing gloom of the overcast day.

"This place gives me the creeps," Trixie whispered. "Too quiet."

"Listen," I said, holding up a hand.

A low whistle of wind filtered through the pines, followed by the distant drip of water. The waterfall was nearby. Somewhere ahead, I could just make out the yawning black of a cave entrance, half-covered by brambles and a fallen tree trunk.

"That it?"

I nodded. "Matches the bend in the river near the falls shown on the map. Let's go."

We climbed over the brush and stepped inside the gaping cavern. Once inside, the narrow opening expanded in height and widened to a half moon shaped grotto. The temperature dropped instantly, our breath puffing in clouds as we entered the rocky hollow. Walls were slick with damp green moss; the floor rose and fell unevenly with stones and old roots. Our flashlights cut pale beams through the darkness of the hollow.

I spotted it first: an iron ring bolted into the ground near the back wall. It looked identical to the one beneath the bell tower. Stooping, I inspected the stone markings closer.

"Help me," I said, and together we pulled.

"Ugh! It must be two hundred pounds."

We struggled, pushing and prying. At last, the stone lid shifted, and with a grunt of effort, we slid it aside, revealing a dark shaft below.

A musty, ancient smell wafted up ... damp earth, mold, and something else. Something evil.

I knelt on the ground, pointing my flashlight downward, and gazed into the hole. Inside was a chamber. Rough-hewn. Ancient. Bringing to mind the Hopewell Indian tribes and their burial mounds we had learned about when I toured the Natural Science Museum with the scouts years ago.

Trixie focused her flashlight into the ancient cavity. A narrow set of stone steps descended into the blackness.

"Here we go again. Are we going down there?" Trixie asked, covering her mouth with her hand. Her voice trembled with a slight hiccup.

"I guess we have to if we want to see what's there. Be careful. This isn't some church basement; these caves can be treacherous," I warned in a low voice.

The bell over the door jingled as he entered the shop. Anna stood at a customer's table pouring tea. He turned at a sound from the kitchen and raised his eyebrows at the sight of Colleen carrying a serving tray. Where was Meredith? He spent half his life searching for his wife.

"Hi Doug," Colleen greeted him gaily, as if it was the most normal thing for a school principal to be working in the middle of a weekday in a tea shop.

Anna gave him a curt nod before scurrying back to the kitchen. He followed her.

"Where's Merry?" he asked as soon as he had cornered the older woman.

"Howdy Doug. Merry told me she needed to do something and would be gone a couple hours. Colleen volunteered to cover for her."

"Go do what? Do you know where she is?" he asked, beginning to lose his patience.

Colleen chose that unfortunate moment to enter the kitchen. With one look at Doug's face, she knew she could no longer lie for her friend, especially not to a lawman. She gulped and cast her eyes downward.

"Colleen, I need you to tell me what Meredith is up to. I can see by the look on your face that you know where she is. You better let me know now before your friend finds herself in trouble."

"Oh dear. I wish she wouldn't put me in these positions. I hate being in the middle," Colleen cast a look toward Anna, beseeching her for help. Anna shrugged and nodded toward the sheriff.

"I'm waiting, Colleen."

"She and Trixie are following up on a clue."

"Uh-huh. Involving herself in this case after I told her not to. And where is this clue supposed to take them?" Doug inquired.

Colleen squeaked. "Honest, that's all I know."

"Okay. Thanks. If she calls here or one of you talk to her, please inform her that the sheriff needs to speak with her," Doug stated then turned and stormed out of the shop.

"Oh my!" Colleen whispered. "She's done it now."

"He didn't sound happy," Anna agreed.

The cavern air was thick with dampness and the scent of mold and time. My flashlight cut a pale beam through the darkness as Trixie and I descended the steep steps deeper into the cave.

"Be careful. This stone is slick."

"I still can't believe this is real," she whispered beside me, her voice reverberating softly off the cold stone walls. "We're following a centuries-old map into a secret vault. How cool is that? If I die in here, tell them I wanted a headline."

"You're not dying," I muttered. "But if you keep talking, you might get your wish."

I took out my son's Cub Scout knife from my coat pocket and scratched an X on the rocky floor with the blade.

Trixie raised a questioning eyebrow at me.

"Marking the trail, in case we get lost. I'm fresh out of bread crumbs," I said with a light chuckle that echoed off the walls.

The path dipped sharply downward. I brushed my hand along the wall for balance. The rough limestone was slick with condensation, and the air grew colder with every step. A drop of water fell from a silvery stalactite and landed on my neck like an icy kiss.

Trixie trembled as a drop hit her in the face. "That better be just water."

"Ugh, what else could it be?" I shivered and stepped away from the rocky wall, etching another X before moving forward.

We walked deliberately, exploring the ancient cavern. I left my trail markers as we went. At one point we had to squeeze through a tight opening between two boulders to go forward, difficult to do bundled in heavy clothing plus a backpack. I had to slip off the pack and carry it in front of me to get through, then strapped it back on.

Ahead, the cave forked in two directions. I held the light over my photographed map, checked the compass, then pointed to Trixie.

"Let's go left." I scraped the X into the floor at the entrance. We slowly crept ahead. A cauldron of bats chattering and hanging above our heads startled me, and I stumbled. My flashlight beam bounced wildly as I thrust my hands out to keep from falling flat on my face.

And there, in the suddenly illuminated dark recess, resting on a flat rock ledge, were two oilcloth-wrapped bundles.

Focusing my light onto the objects, I carefully picked them up, brushing off layers of dirt and cobwebs clinging to the oilcloth.

Handing one bundle to Trixie, I gently opened the larger one with shaking fingers.

"Deeds," I whispered. "We've discovered the original, signed deeds. They're marked with the *Iron Pledge* seal."

Trixie unfolded the other packet. Straining to read the faded ink within the weak light, "Letters. Proof that they knew about the mineral rights. That they meant to protect them."

"Jeez Louise! I can't believe we found them. Now we've got to get them safely back to town," I said as I shrugged out of my backpack and opened the satchel. Removing the two bottles of water, I handed them to Trixie. Then, I tucked the fragile documents inside my bag.

"Let's get out of here," Trixie said and started retracing her steps through the black cavern. Her flashlight cast a weak beam of light within the labyrinth. She made a right turn into the connecting cave and then stopped short.

"Hey, I think you're going the wrong way," I said in a low voice, coming up behind her and not wanting to disturb the creatures clinging above our heads. "Oh no," I said, recoiling. "That smell ... it's ..."

Trixie gagged and covered her nose with her scarf. "Decomposition. Something died down there."

I waved my torch into the pitch-black cave and froze.

There in the Stygian stone tomb, slumped against a huge rock, sat Carl Bradley, alias Harold Foreman.

His skin was gray, limbs stiff, mouth gaped open as if gasping for the last breath he never got. Blank eyes stared. He wore the same blazer he'd had on the day of the museum opening.

Trixie's hand flew to her mouth. Her lips formed a silent oh. She dropped the plastic water bottles. They rolled away. She moved beside me, her voice barely a whisper. "Is he … dead?"

"Definitely."

"Are you sure?"

"Yeah. I've seen enough bodies in the past. He's been here a while," I said in an equally low voice. We both stood there staring at the dead man.

Trixie's reporter curiosity kicked in, winning out over her initial shock.

"Look at this," Trixie whispered, crouching down and shining her light onto the ground next to him. She pulled out a paper caught under his hand. She unfolded a crude, hand-drawn map. It mirrored the map we'd followed, but I noticed one critical difference.

"If he followed these directions, then he went the wrong way at the fork, just like you did."

"Do you think he got lost then?" Trixie asked.

"Perhaps. But why would he come out so ill prepared? I don't see a flashlight or even a warm coat near him."

Trixie snorted. "Not everyone is a scout. What do you think killed him?" Trixie inquired.

"I suppose he could have died from exposure. The inside of this cave gets much colder than the air temperature above. We've had frost and wintry weather the past days. It would have been freezing down here. It's possible."

"Gives me the willies," Trixie whispered.

"We need to get out of here so I can call Doug."

"Uh-huh," Trixie nodded as we backed away.

Hurrying as best we could along the slippery stone surface, we retraced our steps up the narrow stair and climbed out of the secret pit into the open once more. I filled my lungs with a deep breath of clean, cold air and then reached for my cell phone and hoped I had reception.

The ominous sky opened up; the first snowflakes fell, gentle as ash upon the earth.

Chapter Fifteen

Tomb

"What! You went where?! Send me the coordinates on your phone and stay there." Doug raged at me, his voice coming across my cell loud and clear. I glanced at Trixie as she grimaced, listening to the anger in his tone.

"Guess he's coming right away, huh?" Trixie murmured. She shuffled her feet and rubbed her gloved hands together attempting to get warm.

"Yeah, you could say that. He, ah, wasn't too thrilled about our adventure."

An understatement if ever I heard one, I thought. You would think he'd be pleased that we'd found the missing professor or the historic documents. But no ... all my husband could do was rant at me as if I were a child. Jeez Louise! Just once, I wish he'd give me credit for my investigative skills.

"Did you hear that?" Trixie suddenly grabbed my arm and peered into the dark cave behind us. "Somebody else is here!"

"No. You're just letting this place creep you out. C'mon. Let's get out of the wind."

I pointed to a cluster of Canadian hemlock trees with low-hanging branches clutching their evergreen needles. They created a protective canopy. Trixie and I ducked under the boughs and crawled close to the sturdy trunk, huddled together to shelter from the steadily falling snow. Checking my watch, I tried to estimate how long it would take Doug to drive from town into the forest. I hope he took the station's four-wheel-drive Jeep, or he'd never be able to traverse the rough terrain close to the caves.

"Now that we've found the deeds, do you think the mayor will allow me to publish the story about the journal and its impact to Meadowood's history and future?" Trixie whispered. Her breath came out in a cold white fog as she spoke.

"Hmm? I suppose," I said in a low voice. I stood still, concentrating on the surrounding sounds. Was Trixie right? Was someone else here? Bradley's murderer? The hair on the back of my neck tingled. Fear was contagious.

The snow continued coating everything in a glistening white blanket. I heard a hoot owl in the distance; a pair of bluejays screeched, flapped their wings, and settled onto an upper branch of the hemlock. A twig cracked underfoot. I twisted my head around; my eyes searched for signs of an animal or a person. No one.

Stomping my feet, I pulled my collar up and yanked my knit hat lower to cover my ears. Closing my eyes, my mind drifted back to a time in my childhood during a similar snowstorm. I remember dashing outside to play, catching snowflakes on my tongue, and romping in the powdery stuff. Running and jumping, I had followed a baby bunny into the forest behind our house. He was so cute and had allowed me to stroke his soft fur before he scampered away. Following him further and further from my home, I soon became disoriented and hopelessly lost. Everything and everywhere was coated in white; my footprints had disappeared in the falling snow. Crawling under a full blue spruce, I sat on the ground with my knees drawn up to my chin and allowed the tree to wrap its protective arms around me while I cried huge tears of despair. As a child, maybe seven or eight years old, I couldn't determine how much time had passed before my father's voice reached me as he called out my name in his frantic search.

I felt like that now, waiting for my husband to find me. Save me. The enveloping snow, the horror of discovering a dead body... Shaking my head to clear the cobwebs of childhood nightmares, I focused on the here and now. Peering into the dense woods, I strained to hear any sound of Doug coming. How long had it been? Pulling the cuff of my glove down, I read the time on my watch. Soon, he should be here soon. I needed to focus.

"Want a protein bar?" I asked Trixie as I dug into my backpack. "Sorry, I don't have any water. We left the bottles back in the cave." I handed her the granola bar as I ripped the wrapping off of my own. Taking a bite, I chewed slowly, allowing my mind to consider our discovery of Carl Bradley's body ... or I should say, Harold Foreman's body.

Trixie and I ate in silence, the only noise being the crunching of the crisp granola and the wind whistling through the trees.

"You know," I started thinking out loud, "if Bradley died down there from exposure in the cold, who closed that trap door? We had to pry up that stone hatch."

"Oh my gosh! You're right. If Bradley had opened it to explore the caves to search for the hidden deeds, then it should still have been open. He wasn't alone," Trixie gasped as the enormity struck her.

In the distance, headlights bounced off snowflakes, piercing through the dense woods, while the sound of roaring motors broke the silence. Our rescuers had arrived.

. . .

The Jeep ground to a halt. Doug and Doctor Stone stepped out of the vehicle. Deputy Tony Dalton flew across the white powder on a loud snowmobile, then stopped next to the sheriff. He climbed off and doffed his helmet. The three men stood and surveyed the area.

"Meredith!" Doug shouted. He cupped his hands around his mouth and called again.

"Here! We're here," I answered him with a shout of my own as we crawled out from under the massive tree and walked toward the men.

I saw my husband smile, perhaps from relief, before he arranged his face into a proper scowl belonging to a law enforcement officer.

"You've done some stupid things in your day, but this takes the cake. What were you thinking, venturing into those caves by yourself? You aren't getting any younger, you know. What if you'd become trapped? Do you want our sons to be orphaned?" Doug growled as he paced before me.

"Gee, thanks honey. I appreciate being reminded that I'm a foolish old woman!" I scowled right back at him.

Tony coughed nervously, embarrassed by our bickering.

"Well ... I should have known you'd find shelter. Your scouts would have been proud of you," Doug said.

Hmm, small praise, I thought. He enveloped me in a quick hug, then let go as if that was his way of apologizing.

"So show us what you found. How did you know to search here?" He asked, getting right down to business.

"Sheriff? If you don't need me, can I wait in your car?" Trixie interrupted, standing nearby, her teeth chattering from the cold.

"Yeah, sure. Sorry."

"I wouldn't mind some heat either," I said, eyeing the warm vehicle enviously. "How about we sit here for a minute and let me thaw out while I show you the map and explain where Carl Bradley's body is located?"

"Okay. Climb in. You might as well stay warm too, doctor."

The four of us climbed back into the Jeep, leaving Tony to wait next to his snowmobile.

I pulled out my cell phone and shared the photo of the historic map. Doug raised an eyebrow, scowling at the photo.

"How'd that get on your phone?"

"When I helped photograph the journal restoration, of course. It doesn't matter. Just look."

"All right. Show me," Doug conceded.

"If you enlarge this, you'll see the same iron pledge marker near the cave entrance like from the bell tower and journal." I pressed my fingers on the screen and spread the image wider. "When I realized that, I looked closer and recognized the location from all our camping and scout trips into the woods. Trixie and I followed the trail indicated on the map and it led us here. We found a stone trap door with an iron ring attached to it toward the back of the domed cave."

"Okay. The hatch was closed? How did the two of you get that heavy door lifted?"

"We didn't lift it, just slid it off the hole and pushed it aside. There are steep steps leading into the cave below. We followed the trail on the map and it led us deeper into the caverns, descending lower, until we located a chamber with the bundle of deeds described in the journal. It was when we started back to the entrance that Trixie made a wrong turn, taking us into another chamber. That's when we smelled and saw Carl Bradley's body."

"Can you lead us back to that? We need to examine the scene and the doctor needs to transport the body."

"I marked the trail with the letter X along the way; scraped it into the limestone with a penknife. You should be able to follow it, but I guess I can lead the way. I'm not looking forward to seeing that body again," I said.

"Let's get going before the snow storm worsens and we lose all daylight," Doug said, pulling a large LED lantern from the Jeep.

I nodded to Trixie, who smiled weakly and huddled deeper into her coat, content to stay in the warm vehicle.

Navigating with the map displayed on my phone, I led the way into the cavern. Doug stayed close beside me, and Doctor Stone followed him. Tony carried a canvas stretcher, bringing up the rear of our search team. I pointed out the etched symbols on the trail.

"See my X on the floor. This is where the caverns split into two directions. We went left into a deeper chamber where we found the bundled documents. If you turn to the right, that's where Bradley's body is. You'll smell it before you see it," I warned.

The men entered the stone cavity; I hung back and covered my mouth and nose with my scarf. Doug took in the grim scene.

"This is how you found him?"

I nodded as I stared at the gruesome scene again. Flicking my flashlight around the ground, I looked for our discarded bottles of water. They were gone. Puzzled, I turned my attention back to Doug. He repeated the question he had asked.

"Did you touch anything?"

"Hmm? No. Just this," I said, pulling the scrap of paper from my pocket. I handed Doug the makeshift map. "It was laying under his hand."

Doug examined the paper in the limited circle of light, then shoved it into his own coat pocket.

Doctor Tom Stone donned rubber gloves in place of his warmer woolen ones before briefly touching the body, turning the head and placing the body in a prone position onto the unrolled stretcher.

Tony strapped Bradley onto the portable gurney with several bungee cords.

"What do you think Doc?" Doug's voice echoed, the stone wall acting like an amphitheater. "How long do you think he's been down here?"

"It's hard to determine time of death with the body refrigerated, as it were. But due to the amount of decomposition and rigor, I'd say at least six days. I'll know more once I get him back to the morgue." Doctor Stone conferred with the sheriff in whispered words, then stood and stepped back from the corpse.

Doug and Tony each grabbed an end of the stretcher as we retraced our trail toward the entrance steps.

"Do you think he died from exposure?" I asked the doctor as we followed behind.

"No, I believe the bullet hole in the back of the head may have had something to do with that."

I gasped, stopped hiking and stared at the man.

"Keep up, Merry. We need to get back," Doug shouted over his shoulder.

The deputy climbed the steps out of the subterranean cave and then turned to hoist the head of the stretcher as Doug lifted his end from below. I heard Doug grunt with the effort, proving that old adage about *dead weight.*

The doctor and I rushed to ascend the frigid depths. Tony and Doug carried the body to the back of the Jeep, flipping down half of the split back seat to create cargo space. They slid the stretcher in.

Trixie shuddered. "Ugh! I guess I have to sit next to that, huh?"

Doug grinned. "Nothing like being up close to get your facts correct. As a reporter, I'm sure you appreciate that."

"Really? Thanks a lot. But this is a little too close for comfort," Trixie complained, then pulled her scarf over her mouth and nose and leaned as far away from the body as possible.

"I'll hitch a ride behind Tony on the snowmobile as far as the park where I left my car," I told Doug and Trixie.

"All right. You sure you're okay? Be careful driving home. The roads were getting slick when we came out and they're probably worse now," Doug said, then gave me a kiss on the cheek.

I shot him a weak smile. "Hey ... you be careful too. Trixie and I think we heard someone else in the caves and maybe while we waited on you. I'm not sure; it was just a feeling."

"Got it."

"So, I'll see you at home later. I'm planning on a long, hot shower to thaw out these old bones."

"Sounds like a good idea. Wish I could join you," Doug said with a wink and a lop-sided leer.

I playfully punched him in the arm, then climbed behind Tony on the snowmobile.

Doctor Stone sat in the Jeep's front passenger seat, warming his hands over the car's heater vent. Doug took another brief look around before he walked to the driver's side of the Jeep, then paused, and stared back at the cave entrance.

I knew just what he must be thinking ... the same thoughts had run through my mind. Who shot Bradley and closed that stone hatch, entombing his body?

Chapter Sixteen

Homecoming

W hen I got home, a welcoming committee met me, crowding my kitchen, really more like a firing squad. Aunt Fran paced back and forth with her arms crossed while Anna served grilled cheese sandwiches to Billy and Johnny seated at the counter. Colleen stood next to the perking coffee pot as I came through the door and shucked my snowy boots. Everyone spoke at once, their voices blending into one collective chorus.

"There you are!"

"Whatever possessed you?"

"It's about time!"

"Gosh Mom, we were worried!" exclaimed Billy.

Leaving my coat and gloves in the laundry room, I dropped my bags and rushed to hug the boys.

"I'm sorry I made you worry. I was fine. Really." I smiled at Colleen. "I'd sure appreciate a cup of that hot coffee, though."

Colleen poured a mug and slid it to me. I wrapped my hands around the hot cup and savored its rich aroma before gulping some of the hot liquid. I didn't even care if it burned my tongue; it tasted so good.

"Trixie and I weren't in any danger. Though it was extremely cold in the caves and then later when it snowed. We would have been home earlier if we hadn't waited for Doug to join us at the site," I continued my tale.

"What did you find out there?" asked Fran. "Doug and Tony tore out of town without a word when they got your call."

Colleen sidled closer to Anna and cast a sheepish look my way. I knew that expression all too well from our past adventures.

"Colleen, what did you do?" I asked, temporarily avoiding my aunt's question.

"Doug came into the tea shop looking for you. I'm sorry but I couldn't lie to him. I told him you and Trixie were investigating," Colleen admitted in a whisper.

I wrapped my arm around her shoulder in a quick hug.

"It's okay. I left him a message on the counter telling him where I went. He should have seen it unless ..." I eyeballed Mittens and the shred of paper near his food bowl. "Mittens! Did you play with my note?" Reaching for the scrap of paper, I flattened the balled-up missive and laid it on the countertop.

"Exhibit A. Guess you can show that to Doug. Maybe it will keep you out of the dog house," laughed Anna.

"So what were you and your junior partner in crime doing out in the woods?" asked Fran.

"We followed the trail shown on the journal's map. When I had studied that map earlier, I recognized the cave markings and that location. Our scouts used to camp near there. So Trixie and I hiked through the forest and found the caves. It wasn't snowing when we left. All we did was follow the trail on the map and it led us to a secret stone entrance to the chamber with the hidden Meadowood deeds."

"You found them; the documents described in the journal?" asked Colleen.

"Yes. Wait until you see!" I hurried into the laundry room and retrieved my backpack, carrying it back into the kitchen. I pulled out the oilcloth-covered bundle and opened it under the bright fluorescent light.

Heavy yellowed parchment paper contained a swirling script written in black ink. Words appeared faded in some spots, darker on others; the parchment cracked along the lines where it had been folded over a hundred years.

"I want those examined by both a historian and a lawyer," Fran said as she gently unwrapped the parcel and read the first document. Her hand paused over the deed, and her eyes met mine. "What else did you find in that cave? Why did Doug pick up Tom Stone to go with him when you phoned?"

I glanced at my circle of friends and family, then said in a low voice, "We also found Carl Bradley's body. The doctor said that someone had shot him in the head. Doc Stone estimated he'd been dead for at least six days."

Colleen gasped and looked ready to faint. Anna pushed her toward a chair, where she collapsed. I silently questioned Anna as I patted Colleen's hand and worked to bring her around. Anna merely shrugged with that all-knowing smile of hers that made me raise my eyebrows at her in return. I studied my best friend, noting her pale complexion. She seemed to be quieter than usual. Was Colleen pregnant? I might be an honorary aunt soon! I'm sure she'll tell me when she's ready. Hmm, something to think about.

Anna returned her attention to the dusty documents and the startling news.

"Holy cow! If Bradley killed poor Alvin ... then who killed him?" Anna questioned.

My aunt nodded to me, the implication clear.

"We've still got a killer loose in our town," Fran stated.

We gathered the next morning at the town hall. Doug, Fran, and I stood to one side, witnessing the procedure as our new museum director and art expert prepared to open our latest find.

Fran carefully spread the old deeds across the large conference table in the mayor's meeting room, their parchment edges curled and crackled like autumn leaves, the ink faded to shades of rust and walnut brown. The air smelled faintly of aged vellum, beeswax, and something older—like the dust of unspoken truths.

Susan Moore adjusted her reading glasses and leaned over the documents with reverent care. Her gloved fingers traced the iron-ink signatures of Meadowood's founding fathers.

"These are extraordinary," she murmured, her voice almost a whisper. "Hand-penned, iron gall ink, dated 1818. All three family seals are intact."

Meadowood's mayor waited patiently, arms folded, her expression hard to read. "What exactly are we looking at?"

Attorney Gerald Tillman, a broad-shouldered man with silver at his temples and a reputation for discretion, flipped open his legal pad. Tillman had answered the mayor's call and immediately agreed to come to the city building. The attorney and his firm had been on retainer as the town's legal advisors for over twenty years.

"We're looking at a legally binding trust deed—a tripartite agreement between the families of Maxwell, Kirkland, and Johnson. It appears they agreed to hold in common several large tracts of land in and around present-day Meadowood, including parts of the Fox Run Park, the hills east of town, and most notably, the shale field near Fox Run."

The sheriff leaned in, hands stuffed in his pockets. "The same land the fracking companies were after?"

Tillman nodded thoughtfully. "Yes. But this document predates any sale or parceling by over two centuries. And it stipulates unanimous family consent for any transfer of rights."

"Wow, that means the S.O.F.M. and the Ferguson Corporation didn't have any legal rights to make that mining contract last year," I said, recalling the fracking business that had upset the entire town. The same fracking business that Kevin Wyatt had manufactured.

Fran's brow furrowed. "Yes, but until we unearthed these deeds, no one would have known that. Now one of those families is gone; the Kirklands have no living relatives."

"Which is the problem," Tillman said. "With one leg of the agreement severed, no decisions can legally be made. Technically, the land is frozen in trust."

"And what about the other two?" Doug asked. "The Maxwells or Johnsons?"

"With Alvin gone, only Teresa Maxwell remains," Fran said. "She's the last direct descendant. If Alvin had been killed to eliminate his vote ..." Her voice trailed off considering such a wicked motive.

Moore looked up. "Then someone wanted to circumvent the trust. Possibly rewrite ownership entirely."

Tillman looked thoughtful. "We may have another problem. The Johnson family. There aren't any direct Johnson family members that we know of residing in town. We must trace their descendants. If no direct heirs remain, the deeds might be invalidated or absorbed under escheatment law by the state—unless..."

Fran leaned in. "Unless we find someone with a legitimate Johnson claim."

Doug nodded slowly. "We need to dig into the town records. Old census reports, birth certificates, church registries. Someone might not even know they're related."

Tillman tapped his pen against the table. "If any of them prove they're direct descendants, they would inherit a portion of the land rights. The Kirkland estate already deeded its land to the Ohio State University and the Veterans' Affairs. With Teresa Maxwell holding another share, the balance of power and ownership in Meadowood could shift overnight."

Fran's eyes narrowed. "And people aren't always at their best when money's involved."

Silence settled over the room like dust.

Doug cleared his throat. "We need to be careful how this gets out. If folks catch wind that farmland and mineral rights could be worth millions ..."

"It'll divide the town," Fran finished. "Or worse."

"I'll keep the deeds secured at the station with the journal," Doug said.

Tillman flipped another page. "If this goes public, we'll need the entire town council involved. And the state land office. Possibly a court-appointed arbitrator. This is bigger than one museum and a murder."

I stared at the lawyer and considered his warning.

Fran sighed, her voice low. "Then we need to be ready. The ghosts of Meadowood's past aren't finished with us yet."

Outside, a cold rain fell, melting the snow that had blanketed rooftops and turning empty streets into a slushy mess. But within the walls of town hall, the heat of old ambition and buried secrets was just beginning to rise.

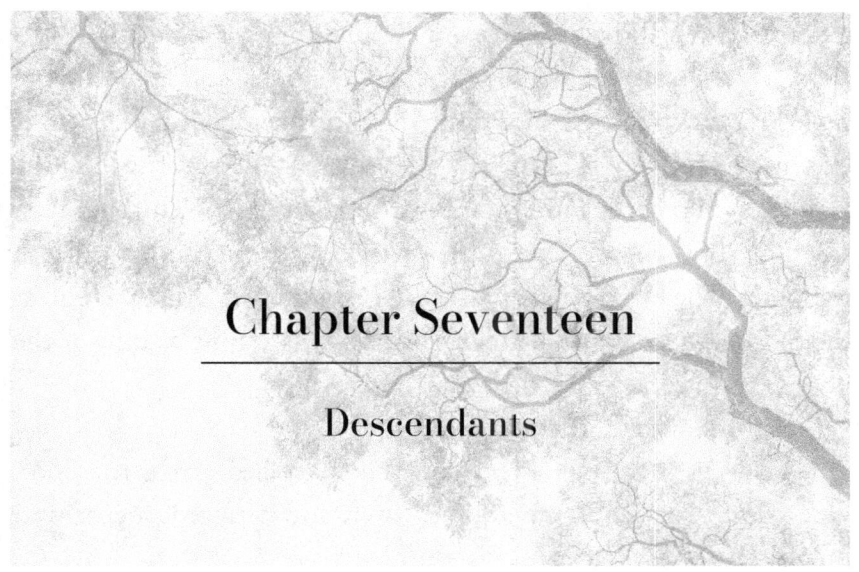

Chapter Seventeen

Descendants

I should have felt satisfaction after what Trixie and I had found in the cave, but instead I'd been jumpy for days — like a shadow was following me just out of reach. All of Meadowood was simmering, waiting for the next shoe to drop. Not knowing where, had me on edge.

Georgia Simmons burst into the tea shop that morning and confronted me in front of a full room of customers.

"Is it true? I heard you found Carl Bradley's body. Did you kill him?" She cried, her face turned a blotchy red.

"What?! Of course not. Trixie and I found his body in a cave, but we certainly had nothing to do with his death. If you want to know more, talk to the sheriff's department. Jeez Louise, you're so upset. It's not like he's your relative." I pushed past her with a tray full of food. "If you don't mind, I'm busy."

She stormed out of the shop and slammed the door. I could only shake my head and wonder what trouble she would cause next.

Later that Thursday afternoon, I came home from a busy day at the shop, arms full of groceries, and my head full of town gossip.

After Georgia's histrionics, everyone wanted to talk about how Carl Bradley was really Harold Foreman, a criminal, and how he had fooled the town council into hiring him for the museum director. It became the topic of the day. No one seemed at all surprised that he had wound up dead, and I found that thought more disturbing than anything. But when I opened the back door, the house was quiet ... too quiet. The boys were at basketball practice, and Doug was still at the office, yet the atmosphere felt off. Mittens wasn't waiting at the door like usual, begging for his cat treats.

I stepped into the kitchen and froze.

A drawer hung half-open, its contents spilled across the floor. One of the bar stools was toppled over, and a jagged line of wet, muddy footprints tracked across the tiled floor.

I set the groceries down on the counter and then looked at the mess in dismay.

"Mittens?" I called, heart hammering.

He meowed from under the table, curled into a ball, his ears pinned back.

"Hey boy. You okay?" I whispered as I cuddled him to me. He purred in reply.

Grabbing a solid wooden rolling pin, I did a slow circuit of the house, checking each room. No one was there. I couldn't tell if anything had been stolen, but they had definitely rummaged through everything. My antique secretary desk in the living room's corner was open, papers scattered on the floor. In the hall closet, the coat rack was nudged aside, as if someone had been searching behind it. The Kincaid painting we had purchased for our fifth anniversary many years ago now hung crooked above the fireplace. A pair of my grandmother's antique brass candlesticks flanked it on the mantle. One lay on its side.

I glanced about our home with its cool sage green upholstered sofa, matching draperies, and pair of light tan recliners in the living room. The sage and tan tweed side chair had been knocked over. My normally homey living room had become a crime scene.

I grabbed my phone and called Doug.

"Come home. We've been broken into." I couldn't keep the slight tremble out of my voice.

"Don't touch anything," he said. "I'll be there in five."

He arrived with Tony Dalton and did a patrol around the perimeter of the house and throughout each room. They dusted for prints, took photos, and confirmed that nothing vital was stolen.

"Whoever it was," Doug said, "they were looking for something specific."

I nodded. "They think we still have the documents from the cave."

"Except we don't," Doug said. "They're in the gun safe at the station. No one knows that except Fran, Attorney Tillman, and Susan Moore."

"But this proves my instincts were right. There was someone else in those caves and he was spying on us. I felt his presence; so did Trixie. He knows I found those deeds."

"He's guessing," Doug said. "I don't like the fact that he's getting bolder." He gave me a worried look and dragged his fingers through his rumpled hair.

The next morning, I met Trixie and Anna at the tea shop before opening and informed them of our break-in.

"I didn't sleep a wink," I said, wrapping my fingers around my mug of chamomile.

"Was anything stolen?" Anna asked.

"No, but someone searched the house. Left muddy prints all over my floors and scared poor Mittens half to death. It took Doug and me half the night to get the house cleaned up and put back in order."

Trixie leaned forward. "First my newspaper office and now your home. You think the break-ins are connected to the deeds?"

I nodded. "Absolutely. Someone's looking for them. Maybe they think we brought them home after leaving the cave."

Anna frowned. "Could it be Carl Bradley's killer?"

"Could be. Who knows?" I said. "The list of suspects is growing longer. What if Bradley didn't kill Alvin and someone else killed them both? Doug only has circumstantial evidence on Bradley for Alvin's death. Without a confession, he can't be positive. Plus, I just can't forget Byron Adams. I'm suspecting anyone associated with that museum. The place seems cursed."

Trixie's brow furrowed. "Adams ... the guy who quit the museum director job? What do we know about him?"

I thought back. "Aunt Fran mentioned seeing him at Alvin Maxwell's funeral. She wasn't certain because he disappeared in a flash. He's supposed to be up in Boston, not roaming around in Meadowood."

"Which doesn't mean he's guilty of murder," Anna said, "but it's strange."

"We also can't rule out others," I said, ticking off fingers. "Kevin Wyatt has ties to finance and land records ... he's back in town and asking questions about land records at the city building. I spoke to him and you know there's bad blood between us. That retired surveyor, Clark Penner, is suddenly interested in property maps again and snooping around. He spoke to me at the funeral and warned me about people deserving recognition; didn't make much sense. I can't even trust Attorney Gerald Tillman. He's always evasive when we ask about the legal implications. What's he plotting?"

"And don't forget Betty's boyfriend Denny," Trixie added. "He was snooping around the museum before the break-in."

Laughing at the absurdity of Trixie's claim, "You can't be serious! Denny Wilson might be a petty thief but he's no killer. You're barking up the wrong tree with him."

We fell silent, tension thick between us.

"So what do we do?" Anna asked.

"We keep digging," I said. "Don't you see? Remember the warning message I found? The *Iron Pledge* is the pact the founding members signed to protect the town, but greed is threatening it. We found the *Silent Bell* that guided us to the journal that ultimately led us to the deeds. Now we have to learn the identity of the *Steward in Shadow*."

"That's right. The warning said not to trust the steward," Anna said.

"Yeah, but who or what is the steward?" asked Trixie in a low voice, with a cautious look over her shoulder.

"We've got to finish the genealogy search and find out exactly who has a claim. But from now on, we don't risk keeping any research in our homes. Doug's locking every paper in that safe," I said.

Trixie gave me a grin. "You realize we're like Nancy Drew's book club right now, right?"

Anna sipped her tea. "If someone's after those papers, they're going to learn what all of Meadowood already knows: you don't mess with Meredith Gardner."

I gave her a wan smile, though my stomach was still tight. Somewhere out there, someone thought the deeds were their ticket to power ... or riches.

And they would not stop until they got them.

Whether we figured out who that someone was before they struck again was now up to us.

My kitchen had become command central as we all gathered together, poring over laptop screens and hugging coffee mugs and teacups. A plate of apple cinnamon muffins bolstered our energy and reinforced our efforts to uncover the missing genealogy of Meadowood's founding families. Computer power cords crisscrossed the counter, plugged into any available outlet.

I was still coming to grips with the idea that my husband had actually requested my help. It wasn't something he did very often. Usually, it was because he had hit a dead end with the case, and grudgingly needed a new perspective. So as soon as we closed our tea shop for the day, I had rallied the troops to help.

"What does Doug hope to find with this ancestry stuff?" Anna asked.

"Motive, maybe. If we learn who the local Johnson descendants are, we might find someone who stands to gain by the discovery of those historic deeds. With Alvin Maxwell being killed, and the Kirkland family line ended, that only leaves the Johnson clan as suspects," I said.

Glancing at my friends, I saw worried frowns of concentration as we tried to track down viable leads. At any other time, an ancestry search party would have been fun. This one could culminate in serious consequences.

By the time I'd brewed a second pot of coffee and laid out a tray of Anna's peanut butter cookies, we were knee-deep in digital archives and half-lost birth certificates.

"You'd think these sites would make it easier," Colleen grumbled, squinting at the glowing screen of her laptop. "I just got six hundred hits for 'John Johnson,' all born in Ohio."

"Try narrowing it down by county," I suggested. "And don't

click on the ones with no photos. That's a rabbit hole straight to nowhere."

Colleen shot me a look. "You sound like you've done this before."

"Sort of," I said, sipping my tea. "I once tried to trace Doug's family back to see if we had any pirates. Closest I got was a coal baron with a fake leg and a bad reputation."

Anna chuckled from across the table, glasses perched on her nose, fingers flying over her keyboard. "Y'all never had to deal with Abilene records. Half of 'em are written in cursive that looks like a drunken rattlesnake got loose with a quill."

Colleen giggled. "Didn't you tell us that your cousin married her stepbrother by accident once?"

"Twice," Anna corrected, popping a piece of cookie into her mouth. "First time didn't count 'cause the preacher got the names wrong. We're nothing, if not efficient in Texas."

I laughed so hard I nearly spilled my tea.

My kitchen thrummed with clicks and murmurs, laptops humming, and occasional exclamations when we uncovered a promising lead.

Colleen grinned. "Hey, remember that time we snuck into the Kirkland barn at midnight to see if it was haunted and I thought I saw a ghost? Turned out to be a raccoon sitting on a scarecrow in the loft."

I winced. "Don't remind me!" I laughed recalling the incident then explained to Anna, "Colleen and I got tricked into doing that stunt on a double dare by a couple mean girls from school. It was either that or lose our lunch money to them. We screamed so loud Mr. Kirkland called the sheriff. Edgar Simmons showed up thinking he had cornered a burglar. We were twelve!"

"I still have nightmares about that raccoon's blazing eyes," she said, eyes wide.

"Uh-huh. I miss old man Kirkland and all the fun we had on his farm. He and his wife sure knew how to throw a party and give the town a good time. Halloween or Christmas, the Kirkland family celebrated with the entire community," I reminisced.

"How about you, Anna? Any thrilling stories you can share from Texas?" asked Colleen.

Anna looked up. "I once thought I found a chupacabra under my uncle's porch. Turned out it was just the neighbor's cat with a shaved tail."

"A what? Say that again," I said.

"Chupacabra. It's a vicious critter. The name means goat sucker in Spanish, with fangs and glowing eyes. Of course it's just folklore, but you never know ... stranger things are found on the Texan prairie," Anna explained.

Colleen and I both snorted at our friend's tall tale.

Laughter rang through the house, and for a moment, it felt like the old Meadowood again—before masquerade murders and bodies in caves.

The doorbell rang.

"That must be Trixie," I said, heading to the back door.

Trixie Jones stood there bundled in a long plaid scarf and carrying a tote bag bursting with manila folders.

"I brought the family tree my grandma started," she said, wiping her wet boots on the doormat. "And a few old photos. She says we have roots in Meadowood. Also have Martha's oatmeal cookies."

"You said the magic word ... cookies. You're officially allowed in," I said, stepping aside.

"Hey girl! How are you?" asked Anna.

"I would have been over sooner, but I had to put the latest edition of the Meadowood Flyer to bed. Paper will be out in the morning. Hi Colleen. Anna. Brrr, it's getting bitter out there. How long you gals been at this?" Trixie asked as she greeted everyone.

"Couple hours."

Trixie climbed onto a bar stool and settled in, pulling out documents and handing them off like a dealer at a Vegas gaming table.

We all began reading the assortment of birth and marriage certificates Trixie's grandmother had saved.

"Let's see what you've got," I said, booting up the Johnson family search again. "Your mother's maiden name was Clary, right?"

"Yep. But her mother was a Johnson. From the east side of town. Born in 1910."

I typed in the data and waited. The ancestry software churned through its digital maze, then dinged with a potential match.

"Well, would you look at that," I said. "Your great-grandmother's sister married a man named Oscar Jones."

I searched through a pile of printouts scattered on the breakfast bar, scanning the information and setting the papers aside until I found the one I wanted. A smile curved my lips as I waved the sheet with its list of names.

"I knew I'd seen that Oscar Jones name listed. Look. Your family information crosses with Betty's. That would make her ..."

"A third cousin," Colleen finished, scrutinizing Trixie.

Trixie blinked. "Betty Jones from Frannie's Frocks?"

"Yes, Betty who manages my aunt's shop. I'm sure you've met her if you've been in the store."

Trixie sat back, stunned. "I'm related to Betty?"

Anna whistled. "Small towns never disappoint."

"Maybe it was fate that caused you to move to Meadowood," Colleen teased.

Trixie leaned forward, her face a mix of surprise and amusement. "I need a minute. This is going in my next column. 'Betty and Me: A Family Affair.'"

I grinned. "Once we confirm the line with a bit more detail, you'll officially be a Johnson descendant. That gives you a seat at the table, Trixie. Along with Teresa Maxwell."

Colleen added, "We still have to verify Betty Jones, but this means the ownership of that land trust might come down to a cousin showdown."

Trixie looked around the room, eyes sparkling. "Only in Meadowood could solving a murder lead to discovering your secret family and inheriting part of the town."

Anna raised her coffee cup. "To bloodlines and bedtime stories ... and cousins you never knew you had."

We all clinked mugs, laughing as the winter wind whispered against the windows.

I sobered as I looked at my friends. The gaiety I felt moments before evaporated like a snowflake in a hot house.

"You know what this means. If the Johnson tree includes Betty and Trixie, and I'm sure it's safe to say that neither of them murdered Carl Bradley nor Alvin Maxwell, then we're back to square one in search for our killer," I said in a low voice.

We stared at each other as the reality sank in. The magical moment of finding Trixie's blossoming family tree had dissolved.

Chapter Eighteen

HB Fuller

Two days passed after the family tree revelation when Trixie Jones received an unmarked envelope at her Flyer office. Inside was a single sheet of aged parchment paper, printed with a 1938 marriage certificate between a Louise Johnson and Henry Clary. Someone underlined the name Johnson in red. At the bottom, a typewritten note read: *"You don't know what you've inherited."*

Trixie raced to my tea shop, breathless, bright red spotting her cheeks from the wintry temperatures that had descended upon the town. "Merry, you have to see this."

Like tea leaves steeping in boiling kettles on my stove, I was steeped in threads of local history. Despite the mayor's or the sheriff's best efforts to keep the newly discovered journal and deeds a secret, the entire town buzzed with the excitement of the historic find. The old deeds had unearthed more town gossip than a church picnic, and half the town sprang to researching their family trees in hopes of hidden wealth.

We sat down at the corner table, hot cinnamon tea steaming between us. Outside, the cloudless blue sky provided one of those rare Ohioan winter days of bright sunshine yet with bitter temperatures. A pleasant change from the gray overcast sky, but I knew it wouldn't last.

"This proves it," Trixie said, sliding the marriage certificate over to me. "My grandmother Louise was a Johnson. This isn't just a theory. It's a bloodline."

I studied the paper, fingers tingling with the thrill of discovery. "That would mean you and Betty are both Johnson descendants—just like we suspected. Only now, it's official."

"She doesn't know yet," Trixie added. "I haven't told her."

"Why not?"

"Because I found this in the archives at the county office yesterday when I was researching facts for a story." She pulled a second slip of paper from her coat pocket. It was a photocopy of a land transfer application filed one and a half years ago. The signature read: H.B. Fuller—but the complete typed name above it listed *Bradley* as the middle name.

"Who is Fuller? Could that be another phony name used by Harold Foreman or somebody else?" I asked.

"I don't know. Whoever he is, he used Bradley as a middle name to tie himself to the founding Luther Bradley Johnson lineage," Trixie said. "He's trying to claim the land by pretending to be the only living descendant."

"But he missed you and Betty."

"Exactly."

I leaned back, heart pounding. "Maybe this Fuller character murdered Carl Bradley because Carl wanted in on the profit. Or what if Carl was trying to blackmail him? Do you think this Fuller was Carl's partner or was it just another name used by Harold Foreman himself, aka Carl Bradley?"

Trixie shrugged. "And now H. B. Fuller is the last man standing filing a claim on the land—at least, he thinks he is."

Later that day, Trixie and I met with Fran, Doug, and Susan Moore at town hall. Susan had called the mayor about uncovering a ledger in the museum's artifact room, misfiled under 'Founding Records - Misc.' Naturally, my aunt phoned me and Doug to join her, and I called in Trixie. The book included pages of handwritten lineage notes from the Johnson family, passed down from a family reunion in 1945. Faint ink noted at the bottom of the page: 'Louise Johnson-Clary, daughter of Luther's youngest son, Samuel.'

Doug spread the documents across the table. "If our killer faked records to support his claim and murdered to cover it up—this just blew his whole motive apart."

Susan tapped a photo in the ledger. "This shows Betty's grandfather and Trixie's great-uncle together. It's all there."

Fran narrowed her eyes. "And this makes them heirs. Legal heirs."

Doug nodded. "And gives motive for this Fuller person to come after them. He'll want to take those documents back."

"I'm not going into hiding," Trixie said defiantly.

"No," Doug said. "But you will be protected, as well as Betty Jones. We're issuing a bulletin for the capture of this H.B. Fuller. And we'll make sure the town council understands who really owns that land."

I sat listening to all the details, my mind whirling, putting pieces of the puzzle together. Fuller, Bradley, Foreman ... so many names, but how many real people? Harold Foreman led a chameleon life, changing his name to suit the circumstances. If Foreman, aka Bradley, was also Fuller, then we had nothing to fear. He was dead ... or was he?

"I'd like to look at that journal and map again. My gut tells me we've overlooked something. Doug, can we go to your office and examine those documents closer?" I asked.

"Not much room in my cramped office for everyone. Why don't I go get the journal, map, and deeds out of the vault and bring them here? I'll just be a minute."

"We'll wait right here, but I want Susan to be the one handling those fragile documents," Fran said, taking a chair at the conference table.

Susan Moore relaxed in her chair, staring out the window as she sat between Trixie and me. Trixie squirmed in her chair. Fran discreetly checked her email messages on her phone. The silence in the room became awkward; I cleared my throat to start a conversation; the sound echoing in the expansive meeting room.

"So, ah, Susan ... have you found a place to live yet? I guess you haven't had much time since opening the museum and what with all the drama going on."

"I've been staying at the Holiday Inn near Pottstown. Other than checking the newspaper ads, I have to confess that I had little chance to look. I've got to find some place soon; staying in a hotel is getting too expensive," Susan commented.

"What are you looking for? A house or apartment?" I asked as a thought came to mind.

"Probably just a small apartment for the time being. I didn't bring much with me. I loaded my belongings into one of those storage units, what little there are. Why?"

"Our tea shop has a really cute one bedroom apartment above it. Anna and I rent it to a young guy who's graduating from college on December 2nd and plans on moving out. He's been a dependable tenant and kept the place as neat as a pin. Would you be interested in looking at it and moving in when he leaves?"

"Well, uh ..."

"Think about it. The apartment has its own private entrance and parking space behind the shop. It's quiet and comfortable, nothing fancy, but the rent is only three hundred a month."

"Wow, that's certainly reasonable and I couldn't get a shorter commute to work." I could see her reconsidering. "I'd love to see it. Thanks for thinking of me," Susan said.

"Great. Sounds like a solution for both of us."

I turned at the sound of Doug returning with a large briefcase in his hand. He opened it and withdrew the leather journal and packet of documents. Carefully placing them on the table for inspection, we all moved closer to Susan Moore as she donned a pair of white cotton gloves.

"What did you want to see first?" asked Susan.

"The map. Trixie thought she noticed another symbol on the map showing the *iron pledge*." I said. "Let's see if there's more."

Chapter Nineteen

Spelunking

O ur first heavy snowstorm fell during the night. Temperatures plunged, and the heavens opened up. The weatherman had forecasted a minimum of four inches of snow in the cities and possibly six or more inches in higher elevations. Meadowood sat on the line, bordering central Ohio cities but in the more rural hilly regions of the county. I knew from past experience, we would feel the brunt of the storm with the deeper snow. By morning, I woke up to a glistening wintry wonderland. Deep snow coated rooftops and deck railings. Gazing out the window, I saw only a few tire tracks marking the snow-covered street.

I cooked a pot of oatmeal and a pan of apple-cinnamon muffins for breakfast. The smell of freshly brewed coffee brought Doug into the kitchen as he followed his nose.

"You're up early. It's barely six o'clock," he said as he planted a morning kiss on my lips.

"Mmm, I couldn't sleep. When this snow stops, I think we should investigate that clue from the map. I want to get out to Fox Run Park today as soon as it clears."

"I don't want you exploring those caves again by yourself. If you insist on pursuing this crazy idea, I'm going with you. We'll take Tony's snowmobile," Doug said as he sipped his coffee and reached for a hot muffin.

I smiled and nodded in agreement.

Writing a note for Billy and Johnny, I set it inside a pair of cereal bowls where Mittens wouldn't find the paper, telling them to eat the oatmeal and muffins for breakfast and to stay inside until we got back home.

Dressed in layers of thermal underwear, a heavy sweater, and ski pants, with a down-filled ski parka over it all, I slipped on waterproof ski boots over heavy wool socks as I prepared to go out. I grabbed my knit hat and two pairs of gloves. Next, I packed my trusty backpack with bottles of water, some protein bars, a flashlight, first aid kit, compass, and the copy of my map that had led me to the caves before. I didn't plan on taking any chances venturing out in this kind of weather, even if Doug was accompanying me. Winters in Ohio could be brutal and a person learned to respect them or risk peril.

Doug drove to the sheriff's office then returned, borrowing Tony's four-wheel-drive Ram truck loaded with the snowmobile and ramps in its bed. I climbed into the cab and placed my pack at my feet.

"Nice of Tony to lend us his truck too. Did you leave him the keys to your vehicle?"

"Yeah. He's good, plus he's got the Jeep at the station to drive. Let's get going," Doug said as he put the truck into gear and we slowly made our way through the snowy streets of town and headed east to the Fox Run Park.

The stillness of the early hour, the weight of the heavy snow bending branches, gave the park an eerie quality ... as if time had stopped. We parked the truck, then attached the ramps to the tail gate. Doug inched the sled out of the large truck, down the ramps.

Doug and I both donned helmets. He fired up the engine, and I climbed on, straddling the rear seat.

"Ready?" Doug asked.

I nodded affirmatively as I wrapped my arms around his waist, holding on as he put the machine in gear and we leapt forward.

The roar of the snowmobile broke the sacred silence of the still forest as we skipped across the snowy trail. We wove in and out of stands of trees. I saw rabbits scampering across the crusty snow as we sped by them. Deer waited behind the protection of the wooded copse.

Wind cut sharp as a blade across my cheeks as I pulled my scarf tighter across my mouth and nose while I clung to Doug's back. The snowmobile plowed into the shadowed perimeter of the park. Snow drifted over the forest path; the wind covered our tracks as quickly as we made them. We pressed on toward the caves near the river's edge.

My mind kept reviewing yesterday's discussion. I pictured the map in my mind, reliving the exploration of the hidden caves where Trixie and I had found Bradley's body. And now I was hurtling toward those caverns again.

Trixie's theory had been wild, almost laughable, but she was right. When I studied the journal map again, I noticed something we'd all missed: a secondary tunnel entrance lightly drawn beneath the old oak grove on the park's north edge. It matched the strange terrain I'd remembered as a kid—the one with the sunken hollow we used to call *Devil's Dip*. The one my parents had warned me to stay away from.

"Maybe I should've let Tony handle this," I muttered, ducking my head beneath a snow-crusted branch. "It's too cold for sleuthing."

Doug spoke over his shoulder, shouting above the motor noise, "Don't tell me you're chickening out. Since when did a little snow and cold keep you from getting involved? At least I don't have to worry about you being out here by yourself."

I shouted, "I'm not so foolish to come out alone; one of the girls would have come with me. But I admit to feeling safer with my big strong husband as my bodyguard." I laughed.

Overhead, a pair of bright red cardinals took flight, and a squirrel ran up the trunk of a sturdy oak tree as we sped by.

We pushed deeper into the forest until Doug slowed and paused beside a rock outcropping partially buried in snow. He shut down the ski-doo, and we climbed off. Examining the markings on the map and comparing them to the rock outcropping, I nodded. Beneath it, barely visible, was a wooden trapdoor, covered in moss and nearly frozen shut.

"This is it," I said.

Doug knelt, brushed away the snow, and pried the latch open with a grunt. A rush of air rose from the tunnel below ... musty, damp, and faintly metallic. The scent curled into my nose like forgotten copper pennies.

"Ladies first?" he joked, but his hand was tight on my shoulder.

I shook my head. "You've got the gun. I've got the flashlight. You go first. I'll light your way."

The wooden ladder creaked beneath my boots as I descended into the narrow shaft. My light swept across packed dirt and rough stone. It looked different from the cave that Trixie and I had explored. Thick wooden beams lined the walls and stretched across the ceiling. We were back in the underworld of Meadowood, but unlike the natural caves, this tunnel was manmade.

Water dripped from above. The rocky floor was wet, frozen. My boot slipped on a patch of ice, and Doug reached out to steady me.

"Thanks," I whispered. "Glad I brought you along." I gave him a wide smile and batted my eyes at him.

"Uh-huh. Just watch your step."

The tunnel branched left and right. To the left lay the entrance to the familiar cave where we had found Carl. My light shone on the letter X that I had scratched into the rock. But to the right, black depths stretched before us; the air felt untouched. An ominous premonition swept over me.

We crept forward in silence, every footstep echoing in the stone tomb-like cavern. A low whoosh of wind followed us from above, like an open flue in a chimney, but it was the silence that made my stomach twist. No birdsong. No distant sounds of the river. Just our breath and the crunch of loose gravel beneath our boots.

"Stop," I whispered, tugging on Doug's arm. "It feels weird down here. I don't like it."

Someone else was down here. I pointed into the oblivion.

Doug followed my gaze. Ahead, a faint light flickered, a tiny glimmer, but unmistakable.

Then I heard it ... a scuff of boots, echoing off the rocky walls. A shadow moved in the far tunnel, heading out of the light.

I ran impulsively, flashlight in one hand, the other clutching my weapon ... a can of mace.

"Who's there?" I called.

No answer. Just the crunch of retreating steps.

I turned to Doug. "C'mon hurry! We've got to catch him."

"Merry, don't ... wait!"

I was already moving, heart pounding. Doug raced behind me. The tunnel narrowed, then opened into a new cavern where a lantern rested on a rocky ledge. In the center, someone had set up a camp table holding a folder filled with papers and evidently maps of Meadowood and the surrounding county land.

But the man himself was gone. Whoever was hiding down here had fled.

I scooped up the papers and grabbed the folder, clutching it to my chest.

Doug entered the area, scanning the surroundings with his flashlight. He noted the bottles of water and satchel containing MREs, meals ready to eat, like the Army issued. Whoever had chosen this place for a hideout had come prepared but likely had not expected the early snowfall. The cave temperatures had dropped below freezing.

"I don't see any evidence of a campfire," I said in a low voice. "Do you think someone slept here?"

"I caught that too. Only a madman would try to hide in a place like this," Doug said. "All right. I've seen enough. Let's get back to the surface."

We retraced our steps through the cavernous maze. It seemed to take longer to find our way out. Finally ... relieved when I heard the water drops plopping on the flat rock surface, a sign we were near the entrance.

"I'm gonna call Tony as soon as we gain the surface and tell him we found our suspect's hideaway."

Doug reached for his radio but had no signal in the cave. Suddenly, a loud crack split the air.

The tunnel shook.

"Look out! Run!" he shouted.

I turned just as the ceiling above gave way. Stone and dirt crashed down. Doug fell hard with a shout, pinned by debris.

I screamed. My voice reverberated in the tunnel.

A cloud of dirt and dust rose into the air as the loose stones stopped falling. The rockslide ended, but I wondered for how long. Was the tunnel unstable, or had someone caused that cave-in?

"Doug!" I dropped beside him, heart hammering in my chest.

"I'm okay," he gasped, wincing.

I knelt next to Doug and worked to push the rubble off him, tossing rocks aside, and clawing away dirt until I freed his leg.

"My leg. I don't think it's broken. Think my heavy clothing protected me."

"Let me see."

My flashlight beam shook as I swept it over him. Blood seeped through his pant leg where a jagged rock had torn through.

"I've got you," I said. "Don't move."

"Like I could." He made a laugh that ended in a cough. The air was full of swirling dust and dirt.

I yanked off my bulky gloves and dropped my backpack. Rummaging through the bag, I retrieved my knife and pushed items away until my fingers grasped the first aid kit. My hands trembled, and I paused, taking a deep breath to calm my nerves. Using the sharp penknife, I cut a wider opening in the torn pant leg to expose the injury. Using alcohol and gauze pads from the kit, I cleaned away blood and dirt from the wound.

Doug winced at the stinging alcohol. "Oww!"

"Oh, you're as bad as the boys. It's just a bit of disinfectant."

He gritted his teeth as I continued and didn't make another sound, yet I knew the leg pained him.

The bandages felt stiff in the cold, but I wrapped them tight around his leg, murmuring to him the whole time, comforting him. I was no nurse, but after tending to scrapes and cuts on two young boys over the years, I did the best I could. Satisfied that the bleeding had stopped, and the bandage held, I scrutinized my patient.

"Can you stand on that leg? We've got to move toward the ladder. Maybe we can get a cell phone signal from there."

"Yeah, I'll try."

I strapped my backpack on, then shoved my shoulder under Doug's left arm to offer support. He leaned on me as we limped around fallen boulders and split timbers, picking our way down the path. We took laborious steps, resting every few minutes until I spied the ladder illuminated in the beam of my flashlight.

Doug slid down into a sitting position. Beads of sweat dotted his forehead despite the frigid temperatures of the cave. His breathing sounded more rapid, and I worried about the amount of blood he had lost.

"Stay here and rest. I'm going to climb the ladder and try to call for help. Okay? I love you. I'll be right back."

"Go. Call Tony. He'll know what to do. Don't go off by yourself." His voice sounded weak as he grunted the last words.

Climbing up the rough ladder, I took a cleansing breath as I gained the surface, feeling an overwhelming sense of déjà vu.

Pulling my cell phone from my coat pocket, I looked at the face of the phone and said a brief prayer at the three bars showing for signal strength. I brought up my contacts' list and rapidly selected the sheriff's office. Tony answered on the second ring.

"Tony! This is Merry. Doug's been in an accident and needs medical help. We're at the caves on the northern edge of Fox Run Park. Trixie Jones knows the exact location. Tell her I'm at the second tunnel. She'll understand."

"Okay. Sit tight. I'll bring help," Tony said, then clicked off.

I climbed back down the ladder to wait with Doug. His body shook lightly, from the cold or shock, I couldn't tell. I snuggled up against him to share my warmth and prayed the help Tony promised came soon.

After a while, I heard engine noises approaching in the forest above us. Voices echoed, calling our names.

I gently eased myself away from Doug and climbed halfway up the ladder.

"We're here!" I shouted, waving my arms overhead.

I signaled with my flashlight to the rescuers on top, then returned to my husband's side.

Moments later, Tony stood with Trixie and peered down into the cavern. He beamed his light at us.

"Hold tight. We'll get you out of there."

Doug looked up at me with pain-hazed eyes. "You okay?"

I knelt beside him. "I'm okay. You're okay. And we've got what we came for."

Tony and two EMTs climbed down moments later. They loaded Doug onto a stretcher and hauled him up through the trapdoor. Trixie wrapped me in an emotional bear hug as soon as I gained the surface.

"Thanks for showing Tony the way," I said as I returned her hug.

"You scared me to death. I'm just glad you're both okay."

"We will be."

I turned once more toward the dark tunnel. Whoever was down there can't stay hidden for long. His secret was now exposed, and soon we'd learn his true identity.

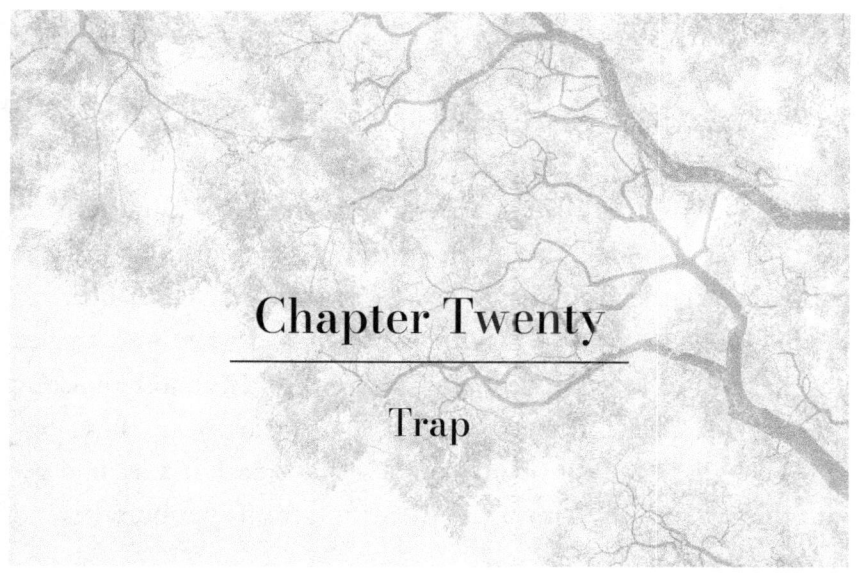

Chapter Twenty

Trap

Doug growled his displeasure over riding in a wheelchair as I pushed him down the hallway of the urgent care center. The doctor had administered a booster tetanus shot and four stitches to close the leg wound. Overall, Doug was lucky the doctor didn't admit him to the hospital for an overnight stay.

"Stop complaining. Be glad you're going home. The doctor told me that if it wasn't for my expert medical care on site, that leg could have become infected. So no more grumbling," I said with a laugh. A smile spread across my face. I couldn't hide my relief that my husband's injury wasn't worse. Of course, I was also pleased that my efforts had been acknowledged too.

"Yes, nurse. If you only knew how much I hate being fussed over and sitting in this wheelchair makes me feel like a namby-pamby," Doug told me in a low voice.

"Everyone knows your not, so quit it. If the situation was reversed, you'd expect me to follow doctor orders and stay off that leg."

"Yeah well, that's different."

"Oh it is, is it? Mister, you've got a short memory where my abilities are concerned," I said, losing my grin and becoming miffed.

I was tired, hungry, and losing my patience with his nonsense. A gal could only take just so much. I parked him in the vestibule while I ran outside to bring the car up to the door. A few minutes later, Doug stood up and limped over to the SUV. He hopped up into the passenger seat, then laid his head back against the seat and sighed.

Billy and Johnny were waiting in the kitchen when we straggled in. They rushed to their father, hugging him tightly, almost knocking him off his feet. Their youthful faces showed anxious tear stains.

"Hey guys, give your dad a hand with his coat and let him get into the living room. I'm sure he needs to get off that bum leg and elevate it in the recliner," I said.

Doug nodded and shot me a grateful look as his solicitous sons rushed about, bumping into each other in their eagerness, covering Doug with an Afghan blanket and bringing him the TV remote. The two most important things they could think of. Mittens jumped up onto Doug's lap to keep him company, his purring audible.

My family was all around me, back to normal. I smiled as I fixed bowls of chicken noodle soup for all of us and took Doug a mug of hot coffee.

Guess we'll leave playing Indiana Jones to the professionals the next time a historic object needs to be recovered in a cavern.

I had an idea I needed to bounce off Doug, but it could wait until tomorrow. Glancing into the living room, I watched him nod off, warn out by the hours of pain and the effects of the medication the doctor had injected.

Tony and Doug huddled in my living room. Doug had insisted on working, and I had insisted he stay home at least one day to recuperate. His deputy took it upon himself to create a compromise by bringing the work to Doug. The papers I had seized during our tunnel exploration were spread out across our coffee table.

With protective gloves on, the men inspected each paper, then placed them into a large envelope along with the hard folder I had grabbed. A replica of the map I had used to navigate the cave system and copies of deeds printed from county archived records were among the stack assembled.

"You know what to do. Dust that folder and each page for prints and run whatever you find through AFIS. If you can't get a match, try the FBI's integrated national fingerprint system. I've got a friend in the Columbus office of the bureau and he owes me a favor. I'll phone him if we need to use their system. We've got to get an identification on this guy. He's been a ghost too long." Doug said in a firm voice.

"Yes sir," Tony answered, then got ready to go.

"And Tony ... thanks for coming to my rescue yesterday. You're doing a great job holding down the station. I won't forget it."

"Thanks Boss. I'll call you as soon as I get a result."

It was late afternoon; I'd just come home from the tea shop. Anna had insisted she didn't need me, but I felt obligated to at least work half the day. The shop was busy with tourists and holiday shoppers. I was glad I had gone in to work; it took my mind off this ghastly business with secret caves and killers running loose. As soon as closing time came, Anna hustled me out and sent me home to nurse my injured husband.

Doug's cell phone rang just as I was starting a pot of spaghetti for supper. He had dozed off in his recliner, his bandaged leg elevated.

The ringing woke him, and I saw him grab the phone off the side table.

"Uh-huh. Okay. Great. Put out a BOLO." He listened for a few minutes then said, "Good work Tony."

I waited for him to end the call, standing in the doorway of the living room, wiping my hands on a dish towel.

"Don't keep me in suspense. Did you get a match on the prints?"

"Yeah. We did. Byron Adams."

"What?! That's the guy Aunt Fran had hired to be museum director originally. She said he quit because of a better offer in Boston. Jeez Louise! Wait until she hears. You know she told me she thought she saw Adams at Wagner's Funeral Home. She only got a glance and wasn't sure it was really him."

"I don't know if he was working with this Bradley or they were in competition, but he's got to be our killer. Now we just need to figure a way to trap him."

"Tomorrow is soon enough," I said. "You'll need time to put things into action."

The moon hung low over Meadowood like a silver coin tossed into a velvet sky. Its glow bounced off the snow-blanketed ground, turning the town into a ghostly diorama of frost and shadows. Pulling my wool coat tighter, I breathed into my scarf. Trixie, crouched beside me near the side door of the museum, gave me a nudge.

"I think my feet are going to sleep. They're tingling. I'm getting too old for this stuff."

"He's late," Trixie whispered, her breath a puff of mist.

"Or too smart," I murmured. "But Doug's betting on greedy and desperate. I hope he gets here soon."

From our hiding place near the refurbished back entrance, we had a perfect view of the museum's unlocked side window, open just as planned. The headline Trixie had published earlier that morning still echoed in my head: *"Legendary Deeds from Meadowood Found- Now on Display!"* A bold lie, but bait we hoped Byron Adams couldn't resist.

Doug had sworn up and down that I was to stay home with the kids. Naturally, I did the opposite, along with Trixie, who practically lives for breaking the rules. We'd snuck in through the party venue's kitchen next door and made our way through the passage connecting to the old parsonage and church. The corridor was cold and smelled of dust and mildew, like forgotten history. A fitting scent, considering the secrets it had guarded.

All of a sudden, a shadow detached itself from the trees lining the church yard. Trixie grabbed my arm.

"There," she breathed.

Byron Adams crept toward the museum, his dark coat blending into the night. Standing next to the side of the building, he paused and looked around. His gloved hand pushed the unlocked window higher, and he slipped inside without a sound.

My heart galloped in my chest. I fumbled in my coat pocket for the small two-way radio Doug had given me days ago, *"for emergency use only."* I clicked it once, the agreed-upon signal. Hopefully, Doug heard it from where I'd seen him in stakeout position near the bushes at the front entrance. If he wondered about the emergency radio click and why I wasn't at home, I'd deal with it later.

Inside, we crept closer to see better, stooping behind a display of antique town ledgers and a mannequin dressed as a 19th-century mayor. My boots made the faintest crunch on the old floorboards, but Adams didn't notice. He was too busy tearing open the locked case labeled "Historic Journal of Meadowood's Founders."

"Looking for something?" Doug's voice boomed through the

chamber, commanding and sharp. He'd entered the building soundlessly.

Adams whirled, the beam of Doug's flashlight catching his face. Panic and rage danced in his eyes.

"You set me up," Adams snarled, pulling something from inside his coat. I froze, expecting a gun, but it was a crowbar. Still dangerous, and potentially lethal, especially when he swung it at Doug.

Doug ducked just in time. The crowbar slammed into a display case, glass shattering like ice underfoot.

"Don't be a fool, Adams!" Doug shouted. "It's over!"

But Adams was already lunging for the exit. He barreled toward the side hall, knocked over a colonial spinning wheel, and kicked open the door to the connecting church yard.

"Go!" I hissed to Trixie. We followed, keeping to the shadows, unseen by both Doug and the culprit.

The church was dark, lit only by moonlight slanting through the stained-glass windows. Adams crashed through the sanctuary doors and ran out toward the bell tower steps in the rear. The same tower where Trixie and I had found the first clue two weeks ago.

"Doug, he's going up the tower!" I yelled into the radio.

The ancient stairs groaned as Adams climbed, each step a protest of age and decay. Doug burst in seconds later, gun drawn, eyes scanning the tower's spiral.

"Adams! Don't be stupid. There's nowhere to go!"

"Better than prison!" came the voice from above.

We all knew the stairs weren't safe; built two hundred years ago from pine now rotten with age. The rickety steps swayed when I had climbed them. Only divine intervention or a miracle kept them from collapsing. Doug started climbing cautiously, and my stomach clenched.

One loud crack echoed through the tower. Then another.

"Doug, get down!" I screamed.

Too late. The upper spiral stairs gave way with a deafening splinter. Adams let out a yell as the boards collapsed beneath him. He crashed down through the air and hit the ground below with a thud. I ran to Doug, who had jumped clear and flattened himself against the stairwell.

"I'm okay," he gasped. "Torn open that leg wound, maybe."

Adams lay groaning near the bottom rail, half-buried in broken beams and dust. One of Doug's deputies rushed in and slapped cuffs on him while the other called an ambulance.

Crouching beside Doug, I brushed debris and snowflakes from his coat where they had drifted in through the broken bell tower window. Trixie stood nearby, her phone raised for a photo, which I swatted down.

"Not the time, Jones," I snapped.

She grinned. "Yeah, yeah."

Doug winced as he leaned against me. "Well," he said, trying to smile, "I guess I'll let you help with the arrest this time since you appear to be in the middle of things again."

"Gee, thanks," I said, brushing a lock of hair from his face. "I only helped bait the trap and infiltrate the museum."

He chuckled softly. "Yeah about that, you and Trixie are grounded."

"You and I both know you'll be thanking me once the paperwork's done."

Byron Adams sat behind bars in a Meadowood cell. He gave up his right to an attorney and broke down, a defeated man.

"Why did you do it, Adams? Was it for money? Did you hope to inherit land?" grilled Doug.

"Money? Yeah, that was part of it. I wanted the power of owning acres and acres of land, but mostly I wanted revenge. Carl Bradley was the real criminal. That's not his real name, you know. It was Harold Foreman."

"Yes we know. Did Bradley also use the name H.B. Fuller, or was that you who filed a land claim last year?"

"No. Not me. Must have been Foreman. We were former associates," Adams said with a sneer. "More like he was the con man and I was the mark but I was too stupid to realize it. He said he was preparing a historical preservation grant and needed access to my family's deeds and trust accounts. But it was all a grift scheme. Instead, Foreman forged our documents, emptied the family trust, and fled. My father had been appointed the trustee of those trust accounts. The bank blamed him for the theft. My old man couldn't live with the shame of being thrown into prison. He died later by suicide."

"So yeah, I tracked down Foreman, found out he was calling himself Carl Bradley. Followed him to this town. Never heard of Meadowood before this. I watched him hit that poor kid on the head too. Murdered the guy. Wasn't anything I could have done to stop him. Guess Foreman's phony identity was unraveling. I don't know."

"I cornered him in that museum and told him I saw some women with the hidden documents. That perked his interest. I lured him into the cave I'd found. When the time was right, I killed him. Foreman deserved to die and I'm not sorry I did it."

Adams had spoken defiantly, then turned his back on the sheriff. Finishing his confession, he refused to say more.

Doug turned off the tape recorder and then walked back into his office. Bradley, alias Foreman, couldn't confess to his crimes, but at least he had a witness along with the forensic evidence to charge Bradley for Alvin's death and close the case. The murderer had become the murder victim.

Dragging his fingers through his hair, Doug sank onto his desk chair. He stared at the wall. So much death. So much grief. And for what ... greed, revenge? Justice might be served, but it won't bring back Alvin Maxwell ... a terrible waste of a promising life

The shadows of Meadowood's past had finally let go of their last deadly secret.

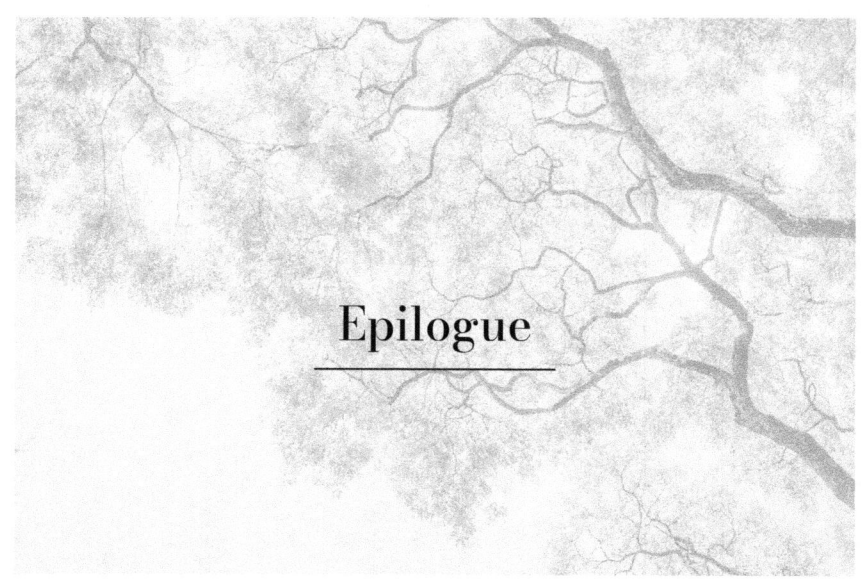

Epilogue

As the truth came to light, Meadowood found both healing and reckoning. Teresa Maxwell, mourning the loss of her brother Alvin, was awarded legal ownership of her ancestral land, a piece of the original Kirkland Tract. Though it couldn't replace Alvin, it gave her a piece of justice, a link to her roots, and a legacy to pass on in his honor.

Trixie Jones, never one to back down from a thrilling story, was recognized across the state for her riveting series of articles chronicling the *Iron Pledge*, the museum murders, and the history buried beneath Meadowood. She was offered a regional journalism award, though she jokingly claimed she was still waiting for a salary raise from the Meadowood Flyer.

Her real award came with the increase of her family sphere by learning that she and Betty Jones were cousins. The girls sat across the table from each other in the tea shop, nibbling spiced shortbread and arguing over which of them had inherited the better cheekbones.

Trixie and Betty had each received a percentage of ownership in the Johnson family land deeded by the town council. The girls had decided to hold the land for future use and prosperity.

The bell over the tea shop door jingled as Aunt Fran swept in, brushing snow off her faux fur collar and stamping her boots like a woman determined to keep winter at bay.

"I swear," she huffed, "this Ohio weather doesn't care one lick that I'm a mayor now."

Anna handed her a steaming mug before she even made it to the table.

"Then sit down and act like one. Hot cinnamon chai and two lemon scones, just how you like it."

"Bless your soul," Fran said, sinking into the armchair near the fireplace. "If I'd known civic duty came with heated scones, I would've run for office years ago."

In all the drama involving the historic documents, the town council applauded Fran, bless her, for her swift leadership decision to replace Carl Bradley with Susan Moore.

Under Susan's direction, the museum not only reopened but was revitalized. School groups, tourists, and historians now wandered its halls, marveling at the very artifacts that had nearly torn the town apart. The mysterious message discovered in Amos Kirkland's desk came to fruition. Meadowood's founding families' pact, the *Iron Pledge*, had been adhered to and the *Silent Bell* had led to the location of both the journal and deeds, while in the end, the untrustworthy *Steward* in the *Shadows* had been revealed. The journal and deed copies now resided within a special airtight case in the museum's place of honor, with a plaque that read: *In silence, truth waited. In unity, truth rose.*

Despite all the drama, or maybe because of it, the annual food drive for the homeless and needy raised more money this year than ever before. The masquerade party ticket sales turned out to be a successful idea. The committee tallied two thousand dollars toward the support of the food bank in time for the upcoming holidays.

I smiled from behind the counter, wiping my hands on my apron. The shop glowed in golden lamplight, snow swirling outside the bay windows like powdered sugar on a gingerbread town. Doug had spent the morning boarding up the bell tower stairs, and now all I wanted was a few hours of peace surrounded by the people I loved.

Colleen arrived last, rosy-cheeked and bundled in a soft green parka. She slid into the seat next to me, leaning in for a hug. "Sorry I'm late. I had a doctor's appointment."

"You okay?" I asked Colleen. I couldn't stop beaming as I guessed what her news would be.

She smiled modestly. "Better than okay." Then she glanced at the others. "Should I tell them?"

"Now I'm worried," Anna said, peering over her teacup. "Is this going to require champagne or Kleenex?"

"Both," Colleen said. "I'm pregnant. Due in May."

The room went still, then exploded.

"What!"

"Shut up!"

"Oh, honey! I knew it all along," Anna drawled. She whooped and leaned over to hug her.

Aunt Fran looked misty-eyed, her hand fluttering over her pearls. "I'll have to stock baby clothes at Frannie's Frocks."

Betty cheered and clapped as if she'd won a game show. Trixie blinked twice, then said, "Sounds like a news-worthy announcement for the paper."

Colleen laughed. "After all the years having children underfoot as principal, I'm going to be a mother."

"I better be the godmother," Anna said immediately.

"Colleen has named me an official honorary aunt," I said, grinning.

Colleen nodded and reached for my hand. "Meredith, you've been like a sister to me all these years. I want this baby to know just how strong, kind, and impossibly nosy their Aunt Merry really is."

I swallowed the lump in my throat and squeezed her hand.

Across the room, the fireplace crackled. Outside, the harvest moon was rising again, casting a soft light over the square. The worst of the mystery was behind us: Byron Adams in custody, the historic deeds recovered, and Meadowood's history museum safe once more. Even Doug had finally forgiven me for sneaking into the sting operation. Although he did tack a "No Trespassing" sign onto the museum's back door ... addressed specifically to me and Trixie. As if I'd pay attention to that!

Betty poured more tea. Trixie grabbed a notebook, "Just in case we uncover a secret baby name scandal."

Anna pulled out her knitting needles, adding, "If it's a girl, I'm starting with a bonnet."

I looked around at the faces gathered there: friends, family, found cousins, and future aunts.

Meadowood was full of old secrets. But more importantly, it was full of new beginnings.

As I refilled the teapot and passed the plate of sugar cookies shaped like tiny snowflakes, I knew one thing for certain:

Whatever mystery came next ... we'd face it together.

Author Biography

An avid reader since childhood, **Nancy M. Wade** always enjoyed writing stories and upon formal retirement in 2012, she decided to pursue her passion. Nancy has written five historical novels, including a western action adventure trilogy called the *"Circle-D Saga"*. A lover of all things mysterious, Nancy created two cozy mystery series. *"A Meadowood Mystery"* is set in a small Ohioan town with amateur sleuth and housewife, Meredith Gardner. There are eight novels to date in this series. The *"Maddie Brooke Mystery"* series includes three novels centered in a historic, southern bed and breakfast inn where recent college graduate turned sleuth, Maddie Brooke, resides with her German shepherd, Luke, and her grandmother's spirited ghost.

Nancy is a member of the Tri-Cities Lost State Writers Guild and is an honors graduate of East Tennessee State University. You can follow her author pages on Instagram and Facebook or her web site at: https://nancymwadeauthor.com .

Also by Nancy M. Wade

A Maddie Brooke Mystery

Innvitation to Murder

Mysteries Beneath the Inn

Death Beneath the Blossoms

A Meadowood Mystery

Scarecrows and Corpses

Deadly Bones

Reunion With Death

Deathly Wedding Woes

Berry Little Murder

Deadly Secrets

Merlot Murder

Subscription to Murder

Circle-D Saga Trilogy

Endless Circle

Moment In Time

Gun For Hire

www.ingramcontent.com/pod-product-compliance
Lightning Source LLC
Chambersburg PA
CBHW070013140726
47908CB00020B/1278